Devil

Black Hawk MC
Book Three

by Carson Mackenzie

Published by CM Books, LLC
Copyright © Feb 2016 Carson Mackenzie
Cover Design by Carson Mackenzie
ISBN# 978-1-952184-30-7
ISBN# 978-1-078746-68-7
ISBN# 978-1-710341-15-7

Synopsis

Lance "Devil" Cummings had put the past behind him until recently when he watched two of his brothers take the fall, bringing front and center everything he had lost. He couldn't be happier for his friends, but for himself - he couldn't deny he wanted what they found–the one person meant to be his solace. What haunted Devil the most was that he'd met her, possessed her, and then let her go.

Bailey Tolson left the bad memories behind when she moved from Shades Valley. When she returned to help her mother recuperate, there was no time to spend focused on the past, at least until he walked in the door of her mother's business.

Two people—one past. One with questions, one with the answers. Can wounds from the past be healed in the present to allow for a future? Join the leadership of Black Hawk MC as they work to get comfortable in their new roles. And watch as another one of the men learns that strength doesn't always come in physical form, it comes from the women who stand beside them.

Table of Contents

Prologue

Devil

With the aid of the darkness, the big willow tree kept my cover as I watched the young woman step out of the house from across the street. The moonlight hitting the porch allowed me to take in her appearance. She looked thinner than I remembered, almost fragile, her skin even paler than before. I was sure if I stood in front of her, that dark circles would show under her expressive brown eyes, the ones my dad had spoken of when I had asked if he had seen her lately. Her blond hair shined in the moonlight as I took in my fill of her.

One year and hundred eighty-two days since I saw her last and held her in my arms. That was when I still had the right to call her mine. I'd stayed away from town the whole two weeks I'd been at Black Hawk on leave, but with shipping out tomorrow, the need for one last look to make sure she was doing okay overcame me, and I'd jumped on my bike without a word to where I was going.

The words she'd said to me on our last day together would more than likely haunt me for years. They already were. I would suffer through it because I deserved every second of the pain. After all, it resulted from my doing.

"I can't believe you're going to be gone a year, Lance," Bailey *said while she made circles on my chest with her finger.*

We laid on a blanket by the lake at Black Hawk, something we'd done a hundred times. It was the place I'd first noticed she was more than just the little sister of a friend. She'd been a sixteen-year-old sophomore and, in the middle of what I would learn later, was the female body in its stages of turning a gangly teenage girl into a woman. I was seventeen and a junior, and if it weren't for my friendship with her brother, James, I would have gone after her then.

By the time the next year rolled around, her a junior and me a senior, nothing could've kept me away from her, and it hadn't. Not the ribbing from my brothers or even hers with the threats of what he would do to me if I hurt her.

"It will go by fast, baby, and then I'll be home on leave." I *pulled her a little tighter into my side.*

"School's going to suck without you there, and even worse, since I won't even be able to see you after the day ends."

"Yeah, going to miss me that much, huh?" She *pinched the nipple her fingers had been near, and I rubbed the spot.*

"You know I am. You being at basic training and AIT (Advanced Individual Training) for three months is rough; a year is going to be brutal. I'll get through it, though, I know that, but it doesn't mean it won't suck."

"Going to suck for me too, baby." I ran my hand over her hip and rested it on her butt.

"You won't have time to think of me, Lance, because you need to spend that time making sure you come home at the end of the tour. I watch the news; I know how dangerous it is there." She raised up and looked me in the eyes. "Between you and James being there, I'll be lucky if I sleep the entire time you both are gone."

As I looked back at her, I saw my future. At eighteen with my whole life in front of me, how was that even possible? But it was what I saw when I looked into her eyes.

"I can't promise not to think of you, but I'll make a deal with you. I'll only think of you when I'm laying down to sleep."

"Fine, and I will think of you before I go to sleep, too. Maybe we will be lucky, and one time we will fall asleep, and it will be our way of being together, even if it is only in a dream." She smiled, and it lit up her entire face. I lifted my head and kissed her lips. Sometimes when she said shit like that, I'd forget how young we were.

"Did you get your application ready for college?" I asked as I broke the kiss.

"Yes. It's too early to mail out, but I have it ready to go. I wasn't sure whether I wanted to go after a business degree or go into nursing. But I finally decided on nursing, so I got the application finished to keep me from going back and forth between the two."

"You'll make an excellent nurse, baby." She moved to straddle me and laid her head back down on my chest.

11

"I love you, Lance," she said in a whisper, and I wrapped my arms around her and held her tight.

Why I held off saying those three little words back to her that night, I don't know, because everything in me then knew that I loved her. Movement brought my focus back, and I watched Bailey as she sat on the swing and moved back and forth, staring straight ahead. I briefly wondered what she was thinking.

I should never have come here. The time when I should have been here comforting Bailey, I stayed away, letting her down because I was too busy dealing with my bullshit. Where did it leave me now? It left me cursing karma as I stood in the shadows, staring at my past, instead of sitting on the porch swing next to what should have been my future.

Pushing off the tree and readying to leave, I froze when her head suddenly turned, and she looked in my direction as if she sensed me. I knew she couldn't see me with the branches of the tree touching the surrounding ground, but it didn't keep my breathing from picking up or my heart from racing as she stood, walked to the railing of the porch, rested her hands flat down, and stared in my direction.

Neither of us moved for several minutes. The thought of stepping out from under the cover of the tree to see what Bailey would do was strong, but the fear of her rejection, or worse, the disappointment I would see on her face, kept me planted where I stood. With a shake of her head, I watched her turn toward the door. As she walked across the porch and reached for the handle, she glanced back over her shoulder one last time before opening the door and going into the house.

It was then that I vowed to stay away because I knew myself well enough to know that I would pursue her, regardless. Because goddammit she was fucking mine, she always would be, and she deserved so much better. Right there was why I would stay away; I couldn't even trust myself around her. I'd had my chance with her and blown it.

Leaving the cover of the tree, I walked through the yards that led to where I parked my bike two blocks away. I ignored the voice in the back of my mind calling me the biggest dumbass in history and that I should be at that door asking her for forgiveness.

But I didn't do it and I already knew I would regret it for years to come.

Chapter One

Devil

The bakery was busy, which gave me the opportunity to look Bailey over as she moved behind the counter, filling orders. I'd stayed away from her since coming back for good. At least as much as was physically possible when two people lived in the same town, knew some of the same people, and did business in the same stores. But I had. I could count on one hand how many times I had gotten a glimpse of her, whether it was passing by as she walked out of the grocery or seeing her through the window of the bakery as I rode past.

Time apart hadn't changed much because I knew from the stiffening of her body that she somehow sensed I was there. She verified that when she stood with the current customer's order in her hands. Her eyebrows crinkled as she looked at me, but then her eyes moved beside me to Ally, and the corners of her mouth turned up. Bailey continued with the customers while Ally and I waited.

When our turn came, and we stepped closer to the counter, and she was in arm's reach of me, that damn voice came back. And as she looked at me and I ran my eyes over her, being a dumbass didn't even come close to how stupid I'd been.

Bailey had curves in all the right places, ones to remind a man about all the reasons he loves females. She had her hair pulled back in a ponytail and rolled up into a net in the back. But I could still picture how it flowed over her shoulders and down her back in waves. One thing was for sure, if I closed my eyes, I could still remember how the strands felt as I ran them through my fingers. When I made my way back to her face and looked into the brown of her eyes, I could see the hurt that laid deep in their depths.

"What can I get you, Lance?"

"How about one of your strawberry cheesecakes and is that an apple pie in the case?" The smile that spread across her face and the chuckle that followed caught me off guard. "What's so funny?" Then I wished I would have kept my mouth shut when the smile faded.

"Sorry, it just... well." At one time, we could say anything to each other. And now, Bailey felt the need to apologize for smiling. "It's what you used to ask my mom when you would come over to the house and she'd been baking. You know when we were..." she paused.

"Dating? A couple? Together? Is it that hard to say, Bailey?" Christ, could I be a bigger dick? But it pissed me off. She felt she couldn't even mention that we'd once been together. And the mad was for me because I was the one responsible for the awkwardness between us. "Is it?" I don't know why I pushed, but I watched the change in her as she stared at me. She clenched her teeth, and her upper lip curled slightly. Then she looked over at Ally, who was busy looking at all the desserts in the case, ignoring us before her eyes came back to me and she leaned in closer. At least as far as the counter between us would allow her.

"Oh no, you don't, Lance Cummings. You don't get to come into this bakery and get an attitude because I couldn't finish my sentence. As a matter of fact, you don't get to have an attitude about anything that concerns me. Your choice, not mine as I recall," Bailey whispered, which I was sure was because of Ally, but she made her point.

"How's your mom doing, Bailey?" She leaned back and stood straight. Her face lost the mad it was wearing at the mention of her mom.

"Good, really good. The doctors cleared her to get back to an actual life. She worked today and seeing her here, well...it was great. With the mastectomy and chemo, they feel they got it all. Time and no reoccurrence will better her odds, but we will take it for now."

"That is good to hear." I smiled, and she nodded. I always liked Claire. She treated me like part of their family when I was with Bailey. I had checked on Claire often through a contact I had at the hospital.

"So... Can I get you the cheesecake and the pie or do you want something else?" Bailey moved over to stand behind the case where Ally stood with her finger in her mouth, in deep thought, no doubt over the selection of cupcakes. It was also Bailey's way of ending our previous conversation.

When I didn't answer Bailey right away, she turned her head in my direction, and her eyebrows creased as I stared back at her.

"Lance?"

I smiled and then said, "Sure, babe, that will be good for right now." The crease in her brows deepened at my words, but she turned and pulled the two items out of the case and boxed them. I battled in my head with everything I had said about staying away. I'd been ten kinds of stupid. Shit, even bantering with Bailey, I'd been more relaxed in her presence than I'd been, for I don't know how long. "Ally, have you decided?" I unglued my feet from the spot where I stood and moved beside her.

"Can I have two?" Ally looked up at me and smiled. As I looked down into her blue eyes, I wondered how the hell anyone was ever going to tell this little girl no. It hadn't happened yet. I was sure life at the MC was going to be really interesting when she hit puberty.

"Yeah, Spider, get what you want." Ally faced Bailey and pointed to the ones she wanted. Bailey pulled them out and placed them in a box, too.

"You comin' to my birthday party, Bailey? I'm gonna be five," Ally said proudly. Bailey chuckled.

"I am. I'm even making your cake." I couldn't help but smile, especially when I saw how Bailey's eyes lit up and her expression softened as she spoke to Ally.

"Yay, what's it gonna be? Momma won't tell me. She said it was supposed to be a surprise."

"Well, I guess that means you'll have to wait to find out then, Spider," I said, and Ally looked at me and put her hands on her hips.

"That's not really fair, Uncle Devil." The look Ally gave me was a familiar one. Speed had used that same look hundreds of times growing up when he wanted the rest of us to do what he said.

"Yep, and trying to get Bailey to tell you your surprise isn't either?" I cocked my brow and waited as Ally frowned at me. I could only imagine the wheels turning in her head. "Whatever you got working in that head, save it. We need to head back, so we are there when your momma and Carly have dinner finished."

"'K. Can I eat a cupcake in the car?" Bailey chuckled, and I glanced over at her and smiled.

"Nope." Ally's head dropped, and I could see her mouth in a full pout. When Sami and Ally first moved to Black Hawk, me or one of the others would have jumped through hoops to make her smile again. That was until Sami and Carly called us suckers, then laughed and informed us Ally had each of us wrapped around her finger. The others and I wanted to argue with the women, but what would that have accomplished? Instead, we all agreed. I, for one, hoped the pint-sized biker chick never learned to tear up, because we would be screwed. "Not going to work, I'm on to you." Jeez, when her head raised and her eyes hit mine, and she smirked. The only thing I thought was screwed wasn't a strong enough word.

"You men are doomed. You know that, right?" Bailey said and chuckled as she rang up the sale. I moved to stand in front of the register and pulled out my wallet to pay.

"You might be right. When I have kids, they're going to be all boys." I picked up the boxes and held them with one arm and reached for Ally's hand with the other.

"It's a 50/50 chance. You're a medic. You should know that?" Bailey grinned.

"Nah, my ol' lady wouldn't do that to me. Besides, nothing but male swimmers," I answered as Ally pulled on the door and I hooked it with my foot and used my hip to open it for us.

"You don't like girl swimmers? I'm a girl swimmer. Daddy's been teaching me." Ally stopped and looked up at me. I looked down, and the look of hurt on her face made my chest ache. Well shit.

"That you are, sweetheart. I just wouldn't want to have a little girl because I would worry she wouldn't be able to swim like you, then her feelings would get hurt." I held my breath and waited to see if I would need a ladder to get out of the hole I dug, but Ally cut me a little slack and smiled.

"It's okay. I will help if you have a girl."

"Well, I see you haven't lost your touch." Bailey chuckled and then told Ally bye.

Ally walked through the door in front of me and yelled goodbye to Bailey over her shoulder.

"Guess I could test it out on an older female." I leaned away from the door, and it started to close behind me. "See you again soon, baby."

The door clicked shut as she said, "What?"

I smiled. Maybe I should thank Sami and Carly for sending me to town after all.

Chapter Two

Bailey

What the hell just happened? I walked to the door, turned the lock, flipped the closed sign, and with the cord to the blind in my hand, I watched Lance as he helped Ally into the truck. Until today, I had only seen him at a distance. Even with the years apart, I felt the second he had walked into the store. The air thickened, my heart beat a little faster, and my skin tingled as if it waited for his touch. *Christ, how pathetic is that?*

Lance walked around the truck to the driver's side and opened the door, but before he got in, his head raised and his eyes met mine. I couldn't turn away. His eyebrows furrowed and as he stared at me, I watched his facial expression change to that all too familiar smirk. Then he winked, got in his truck, and I continued to watch as he pulled away. When I lost sight of the truck, I pulled the cord to the blinds and went through the bakery, closing it down for the day.

He'd filled out from the young man who left and put a crack in my heart. Being close to him again and trying to be an adult sucked. Deep down, I wanted to be the teenage girl who stomped her foot and asked *what the fuck?*

As I got in my car to head home, I thought of the layers of crap life kept dumping on me. After the last few days, with Mom's doctor's visit, which had gone excellent, things looked as if they turned around for a change. Well, until the door opened to the bakery and one of the best and worst things from my past entered.

When I opened the door to the house, the sound of my mom humming, and the aroma of what she was cooking hit me, I shoved the past back into its corner of my mind.

"Whatever you are cooking smells fantastic, even though you should rest instead," I said as I walked into the kitchen and found my mom chopping items at the counter.

"And here I thought I was the parent." Claire, my mom, chuckled.

Cooking had been a love of my mother's, one put on hold when cancer and the treatment had taken her energy away. Seeing her back in her element for the first time in quite a while made me smile.

"Yeah, well, what can I say? I've gotten used to taking care of you." I moved around the kitchen, getting plates and utensils out, and as I set the table, the sound of the knife hitting the cutting board had stopped.

"I'm sorry, Bailey," my mom said, and I turned toward her.

"Mom, I didn't mean anything by that, other than it is going to be hard standing back and watching you do the things I have been doing for some time now. I'm happy you are feeling better and getting back to yourself. I just don't want you overdoing it." I sat the utensils out and then looked back at her as she placed the salad fixings into a bowl. "What else do you need me to help with?"

"Everything is ready," she said as she pulled the bread out of the oven. "If you grab the salad, I will bring the rest to the table." I did as she asked, then we both sat at the table to enjoy our meal.

"This is great, Mom."

"Thanks, honey. Felt good moving around in the kitchen again."

"After we finish eating, I'll clean up the kitchen so you can sit down and put your feet up after working and cooking all this," I said, and motioned with my fork at the spread in front of us.

"Actually, I'm not tired. Getting back to the bakery and cooking again, it's like having my life back. From the minute they diagnosed me, it felt as though my life wasn't my own. I wasn't living. I was just going through the motions. It would have been so easy to let go instead of fighting, but when I thought of leaving you alone in this world, I couldn't *not* fight to survive." She stood and cleared the table.

"Mom, what brought this on?" I asked and waited for her reply.

"I never want to feel that way again. I plan to focus on living. We of all people, Bailey, have had our fair share of loss. James, your dad..." When her eyes searched mine, I knew who else she wanted to add.

"Lance. Is that why you paused? Mom, I've gotten over him. You should never feel as if you need to guard what you say in front of me." I stood from the table and grabbed the remaining dishes and carried them to the sink. "I'm stronger than that. You should know that too. I get it from you," I said as I cleaned up the kitchen.

"Have you, sweetie?" my mom asked softly as she reached for an empty container under the cabinet.

I took a deep breath and squeezed my eyes closed. Why, of all days, did she feel the need to go over this? I opened my eyes and with another deep breath, "Yes, Mom, I am. I've dated several men since Lance. Shit, until right before I moved back here, I was engaged. I would still be engaged or married if I hadn't broken it off with Matt. Before that, I dated Steven, who cheated with someone I thought was a good friend. Did I pine over that?" I didn't give her a chance to answer before I continued. "No, I didn't. So, what has brought this on about Lance?" I stopped what I was doing to turn to look at her. She paused what she was doing and shifted to face me.

"Then how come you haven't seen Sami or Carly since they both moved to Black Hawk? You haven't even been anywhere with Mac, either." Mom's raised eyebrows let me know she noticed more than what I gave her credit for.

"Been a little busy with the bakery and you. We've talked on the phone and even had lunch a couple times when they've come into town. I haven't been to Black Hawk because they're both getting settled in. Mac is busy with her practice, so she has limited free time." It was mostly the truth, but I could tell by her expression that she wasn't buying it.

"Bullshit!"

"Ma!"

"Fool yourself, Bailey, but don't pull me into your denial." We worked in silence, and as I washed and dried, she put the leftovers away and wiped everything down.

When we finished, I went to my bedroom and changed into sweats and a t-shirt before I made my way into the living room. Mom was already there, sitting in the recliner with her feet up, and the TV was on, showing the news. As I sat down on one side of the couch, I noticed a glass of iced tea sitting on the end table. The gesture might seem small to most, but I was supposed to be taking care of her, which at first, she was too weak and had no choice other than to allow it. Not so much as she gradually built her strength back after the treatments stopped. Mom wasn't out of the woods yet, but each day that passed with her in remission, the odds of beating her cancer would grow.

I picked up the entertainment magazine off the coffee table and flipped the pages while I ran every detail from my encounter with Lance through my head. I had no clue what had been going through his mind because I had been dealing with my thoughts. But after my mom made the statement about Sami and Carly, it was all I could think about. Yeah, I was hurt over everything, but I moved on—I survived. The hardest part was needing my best friend, then remembering he was the reason for some of the hurt.

After I laid the magazine on the table, I settled back into the couch, curling my legs up on one side of me just as the news ended.

"What do you want to watch?" I asked like I did almost every night since I moved home.

"You choose," Mom said as she tossed the remote to me. I caught it, and before I pulled up the guide to see what was on, she continued. "You shouldn't be sitting home with your mother; you should be out with friends having fun. Better yet, a man."

I stopped scrolling and turned to look at her. "Ma, really? Are we back to that again?" I lifted my eyebrows at her.

"I'm going to tell you what I think, whether or not you want to hear it."

"Yeah, I'm sure you will," I sighed.

"You don't want to go visit Sami and Carly because you don't want to take the chance of running into Lance at the Black Hawk compound. The three of you hung out frequently until they took up with Kane and Russell. And I know Mac is a recent addition to your little group, but you aren't even staying in contact with her. Now you spend your entire time either at the bakery or here. Sweetie, I'm so thankful to have had you around to help me, but I am feeling better, and frankly, your hovering is getting on my nerves. If you and I have learned anything over the last several years, it is life is short."

"I really am not avoiding Lance, Ma. I'll be going to Black Hawk to attend a birthday party for Sami's little girl, Ally. She invited you also if you're up to it. Plus, Sami hasn't been working as much at the strip club because of moving. Once she gets settled in, she will be in town more often. As for Carly, she is still recuperating, and I don't think she is supposed to be back to work at the station for at least a month. Mac has been busy too. I will see a lot more of her once I get the results of my RN test. As soon as my score is in, I will have an interview and talk with her. And as far as Lance goes, well, he's the one who avoids me. At least that was the case until this evening when he came in with Ally to pick up dessert for dinner at Sami's house," I said it all in one breath, then went back to scrolling on the TV.

"Why didn't you say anything when you came in?"

I sighed, "Because I didn't want to have this conversation with you. It wasn't a big deal. I'll admit it was awkward at first, but I got through it. You know, young love and all that bullshit. Lance went his way, I went mine. Yes, I was a mess when he didn't come around when his training finished or any other time he made it back to town. But I survived that too. The part that hurt the most was not a single word when James died or even Dad. James was a friend to all of them, and we heard from each one except

Lance. Their fathers came to both funerals. Hell, most of the Black Hawk MC came.

"Besides, what did you think when I started dating others when I finally went to college? I moved on. Let's not forget that I was engaged not that long ago." I clicked on an HBO original movie that looked interesting and then placed the remote on the table beside me before my mom said anything in reply.

"Yes, I remember all that. I also remember the guys you dated when you went away to college," she shook her head, "losers. Every single one of them."

I laughed at her expression more than at her words. "They weren't that bad. You liked some of them."

"No, I really didn't. You seemed to like them, so I wanted you to be happy. I went to bed most nights and prayed it was just you sowing your wild oats. And my worse fear was that on one of your visits you were going to announce you were pregnant." Mom took a drink of her own tea before she continued, "That one, ummm... Draper. Good God, Bailey, could that boy even add? I often wondered how he even had gotten accepted into college."

"Be nice. He went to school on a baseball scholarship. They supplied tutors for him. He got his degree and graduated. That was how I met him. I was one of his tutors."

"His tutor in what?"

"Math." We both burst out laughing. I missed this with my mom. After James and my dad died, we had become closer, using each other to lean on.

"You told me you broke your engagement with Matt because you didn't love him enough. I said nothing then because it was the beginning of my medical problems. But did you feel that way because some part of you still loves Lance?" Mom asked and sat patiently as she waited for me to answer her.

"A part of me will always love him, Ma. He was the first man outside of the family I felt that way about. But like you said back then, we were young. He and I need to make some effort toward at least being comfortable around each other because we will run into each other more since I'm friends with Sami and Carly. Maybe he realized that too, and it's why he came to the bakery, to show that he can handle being around me. Doesn't really matter, though. We're adults, so I think we can act accordingly," I left off that I hoped we could, especially after being close to Lance today. But there was no way I was sharing *that* with my mom, so I went on, "Besides, you're getting back to work, and I'm waiting to hear on my NCLEX exam, so all is good." My mom chuckled.

When my mom called with the news about having cancer, I hadn't thought twice about what I needed to do for her. Dropping out of school and being with her while she went through the fight of her life was an easy decision. However, when the school called and told me after looking at everything that I was within reach of my degree, I'd been ecstatic.

I was lucky I was so close to finishing my nursing classes when my mom was diagnosed because they let me complete everything over the computer and, with more than enough clinical hours, it had worked out fantastically. Working as a registered nurse was within reach. I'd graduated with a master's in nursing and now waited for the results from my RN certification exam.

"Oh, sweetie, at your age you should know that men never act accordingly. And we won't even get into a discussion about them acting like adults. Well, at least not when they want something."

"True."

We continued to talk and laugh while we watched the movie. It had been a long time since my mom and I enjoyed a lazy evening together. I pushed what happened with Lance away, blowing it off as reading too many romance books, and placed my focus where it needed to be—getting my life back on track.

Chapter Three

Devil

Sami and Carly kept glancing at me as we ate the dessert I picked up from the bakery. When Ally and I got back, the food was done and on the table waiting, so other than Coast asking what we picked up, no one had said a word. I knew the guys wanted to ask how it went, but they would wait until the women weren't around. From the looks I was getting from the women, though, they knew at least some of mine and Bailey's history, either from their men or Bailey. I'd bet on Bailey since Speed and Crusher would never share my story, even if the women asked about it.

"Can I haves another cupcake?" Ally asked, breaking the silence.

"One is plenty. You can have another tomorrow," Sami answered her as she picked up the napkin and wiped Ally's mouth off.

"Buts Uncle Devil bought them for me. So, can I ask him?"

"Didn't your momma just tell you no?" Speed asked Ally. And I watched Ally look between him and Sami as if deciding how much she could get away with. Coming off the whole collecting money from the men every time they said a cuss word, I wondered if she would push. The rest of us continued to eat but watched the show and with the sigh that came from Ally, guaranteed it was going to be good.

I didn't know if it was because Ally was so much like Speed or if she just didn't have any self-preservation skills yet.

There was no envy of Speed at all from me, because I figured he was working out how he was going to keep both his women happy. Watching Speed the last couple of months, as he learned to be a father, had been quite amusing to the rest of us. Still was.

"Yep, but Momma don't understand how much I love cupcakes. Sometimes she even gets grouchy when I ask for them." Ally looked at Speed with what I could only call sad puppy-dog eyes, which had Speed glancing over at Sami with his lips pressed together to keep from smiling.

"Ally, take your plate to the sink and then go upstairs and I will be up in a minute to help you get ready for bed." Sami shook her head and rolled her eyes at Speed.

"Don't be mad, Momma, or you going to have to get laid. Right, Daddy?" Ally asked, and I bit the inside of my mouth to keep from laughing. As I looked around the table, the others seemed to do the same while they looked down at their plates.

"Where did you hear that, Spider monkey?" Carly asked, her lips twitching.

"Daddy told Momma the others day when she was mad." Ally turned from Carly to Speed, "What's laid, Daddy?" Crusher's chuckle cut off when Carly elbowed him, and the inside of my cheek was going to bleed, I bit down so hard on it. But I would deal because paybacks were fan-fuckin-tastic.

"That is something grownups say, Ally. Now do what your momma asked you to do," Speed said.

"'K," Ally said and got down from her chair, picked up her plate, and walked over to the sink and sat it down. She didn't make another sound until right before she reached the door and stopped to look at Speed. "I'm never getting laid."

Flirt placed his fisted hand at his mouth and coughed out, "At least not for like twelve years." Coast, Jag, Crusher, and I lost our fight with keeping it together and laughed out loud while Speed glared at Flirt before he turned back to his daughter.

"That is all the better, baby. You not getting laid will help Daddy sleep easier." Sami elbowed Speed, and he smiled. "What?" Speed asked, and Sami shook her head, then focused back on their daughter.

"Ally, don't worry about it. Now head on up, and I will be there in a minute," Sami said, and her parenting skills impressing me because I didn't know if it were me I could have kept a straight face.

"Okay, Momma. But is it like this morning when you told me only big girls needed to pee on a stick?"

"Umm..." Sami glanced at Speed, then looked back down at Ally. "Yes, sweetie. Now go upstairs. I'll be right behind you," Sami said, and Ally nodded and headed out of the room.

My eyes snapped to Speed's face, and it seemed I wasn't the only one who realized what Ally's words meant. The room was so quiet that I'm not sure any of us took a breath. Sami turned to Speed after she made sure Ally had headed up the stairs. Speed's face wore a blank expression as he stared at Sami.

"Say something, Kane," Sami said and sucked her bottom lip in and bit down on it.

"Maybe you should talk first," Speed said.

"Holy shit. Was it positive?!" Carly blurted out, and Sami nodded but never took her eyes off Speed. "Well damn, my brother, with the same skank of a mother, didn't waste any time."

"Nice, sugar. And you elbow me for laughing," Crusher said as Speed pushed his chair back and stood, wrapped his arms around Sami, and pulled her up with him, burying his face in her neck.

"Kane, you're not upset?" Sami's words brought Speed's head back up, and I watched a huge smile cross his face.

"Fuck no, Sami. Never, baby. I'm gonna get to see you get big and round with my child growing inside you. I missed that with Ally," Kane's voice lowered at the end.

"Congrats to you both." I pushed my chair back and stood, and Speed set Sami back on her feet, and I shook his hand, then hugged Sami. The others followed suit, and after everyone was done, we headed out the door to give Speed some private time with his family.

I walked with the others as we headed toward our homes. I was caught in my own thoughts and hadn't realized it until Jag hit my shoulder.

"What did you do that for, asshole?"

"Coast asked you three times if you wanted to ride down to Soft Tails to grab a beer and watch the girls." Jag laughed.

"Nah, I think I'm going to grab a beer at the house and relax on the porch."

"Seriously? You are passing up watching the women shake what God gave them," Coast said, and the others laughed.

"Or a surgeon," Carly said sarcastically, which had us laughing harder.

"You jealous, sugar?" Crusher teased.

"Nope, I like most the women who work there. Most are working as strippers for a reason. It's you men who act as if you've never seen a naked woman before." Carly huffed and continued to walk, but I noticed the slight limp when her weight shifted to the leg she had been shot in. Crusher must have noticed it too, because he stepped closer and put an arm around her waist.

"Ah, now no sense getting nasty because men like to admire the differences in the female body," Crusher said and squeezed her briefly.

"Oh please, feed someone else that line of shit. More drool probably gets mopped off the floor than beer," Carly said and moved out of Crusher's hold.

"Or body fluids," Coast said, and Carly stopped.

"Dude, really? That was kinda gross." Carly looked at him pointedly, and Coast shrugged. "But does that happen? I've never witnessed that when I was there."

"Go to the club often, sugar?" Crusher asked and cocked his brow.

"Hello! My best friend manages the place. I've been there in a professional capacity and to visit Sami. Besides, Perry makes the best fried chicken around."

"In all the times I've been there, I've never seen you," I said.

"Umm... probably because you were one of them too busy drooling," Carly answered me flippantly.

"Nah, just enjoying the view," I said, then laughed when she rolled her eyes.

"Come on, sugar. Let's go home so *I* can enjoy *your* view," Crusher said, and then smacked Carly's ass.

"Fuck, can you have pity on us who don't have the option of getting laid every night and close your damn windows," I groaned.

"No shit," Coast piped in.

"Fuck you." Crusher laughed and bent, swooping Carly off her feet before heading toward their house. We stood and watched them until they entered their place and the door closed.

"Damn, I'm going around to the garage to get my bike. Are we heading to Soft Tails or not?" Flirt asked.

"Yeah, sounds good. You sure you don't want to head out with us, Devil?" Jag turned and asked.

"I'm good with just relaxing here," I said and turned toward my place.

"You okay, brother?" Coast asked, and I stopped and turned back around.

"Yeah," I said, and looked between each of my brothers. "Why?" I asked when I noticed they were all watching me but trying not to watch me.

Jag shook his head. "Fuck, how did it go at the bakery?" Coast and Flirt groaned, and Jag glanced at them. "Don't act like your goddamn asses don't want to know?"

"Fuckin' A, when did you assholes turn into a bunch of women? Wanting to talk about feelings and shit." Flirt acted disgusted at my words but didn't walk off. "Seriously?" I raised my brows.

"Oh hell, just tell us how it went between you and Bailey, so we can go back to doing manly shit again. Like getting on our bikes and going to have a beer at the strip club," Coast said, leaned back on his heels, and shoved his hands into the pockets of his pants.

I looked at Crusher's house and then at Speed's. "Am I the only one who thinks those two are lucky bastards?" It was quiet for a minute when neither of my brothers answered my question right away.

"No, you're not. We would all be lucky to find what they have," Flirt said, then Jag jumped in.

"If I ever take an ol' lady, I hope she is half as strong, smart, and beautiful as Sami and Carly are. Because for every ounce of grief those women give Speed and Crusher, you can't deny that our brothers aren't happy."

"No, you can't. So, if I come across a woman that does that for me, I will pursue her ass until I have her," Coast said and looked right at me with his eyebrows lifted.

"Alright, I get it. Seeing Bailey. Being close to her. Talking to her. It has me questioning if I was wrong in my thinking."

"Devil, after you told us what happened, we told you then to tell Bailey everything. I know we gave you shit when you dated her exclusively in high school. But we didn't know shit then. However, we've never *not* gone after what we wanted. Ever. If you want her, brother. Go get her." I nodded when Flirt finished.

"I feel sorry for the woman that catches your eye, Flirt," Jag said, lightening up the moment, especially when Flirt flipped him off.

"Are we done, now? Can we pick our man-cards up off the ground and head to Soft Tails or what?" We all chuckled at Coast.

"Sure you don't want to go?" Jag asked.

"I'm good. Ride safe, brothers," I said, and turned toward my house.

"Always," was answered from the three as I made my way up the few steps onto the porch, and then into my house.

By the time I took a leak, grabbed a beer out of the fridge, and made it back to the porch to sit down, Flirt, Jag, and Coast were rolling out. I waved and sat down on one of the wooden rockers. When my head was clouded with thoughts, I needed time alone to organize and work through the things that bothered me. I'd been that way most of my life, and it was one of the reasons the others didn't harp on me to go with them.

With my legs stretched out and my feet crossed on the banister, I drank my beer and thought about Bailey. Time apart from her didn't make it any easier to stand in front of her as though she had meant nothing. Could I risk changing the hurt in her eyes to hate if I explained about James? Did I even want to take the chance? I leaned my head back against the house, sighed, and let memories of the time spent with Bailey wash the cloudiness away. Funny how even in my thoughts, she felt like home.

Home. Even as young as we were, Bailey had always been that for me and so much more. I felt the smile form on my face. I might have been joking about only having boys,

41

but thank God the statement of finding out with her hadn't come out of my mouth. When I thought about it, I knew I had made my choice. Even as I talked with my brothers, I knew the answer.

Mine. Bailey would always be mine.

"Hell, do I want to know what's got you smiling like that?"

My eyes flew open, and my feet hit the porch. "Goddammit, Dad!" My dad, David Cummings, sat down in the rocker next to me as he laughed.

"Good to see your military survival skills still work. Not even mentioning what you were taught in the club."

I looked over at him, and his lips twitched. I loved my dad, but he was stuck with the name Preacher for a reason. The man could sit for hours and never say a word. Other times, if he started talking, no one was getting a word in. Thankfully, it didn't happen a lot.

"Yeah, whatever. I was a medic. We didn't have to practice being quiet. We actually wanted the men to hear us coming."

"Less fun that way." My dad chuckled.

"Less chance of one of the wounded shooting us because they thought the enemy was coming to finish them."

"True. So, going to tell me why I caught you smiling?" I looked at my dad, who stared back with his eyebrows raised in question.

For the first time, I noticed the gray appearing at the temples of my dad's sandy brown hair. Hair color was the only difference between our looks. We shared every other feature, from our dark brown eyes and square jaw to height and build. If not for the man beside me, I never would have been born. I sure in the fuck wouldn't have survived after without him.

"Thanks for everything you've done for me," I said, and his questioning look turned into one of worry.

"What is going on with you, Lance? I saw Flirt, Coast, and Jag riding out. Not like you not to be with them. Especially since Crusher and Speed got women to answer to."

"You saying Crusher and Speed are pussy whipped, Dad?"

"Yeah." I opened my mouth, and he stuck his hand up to halt me. "Do they show any weakness for their women? Yes. It's not a bad thing. I might never have had an ol' lady but, son, no man, including a badass, bucks his woman unless he wants to go without *and* enjoys sleeping on the couch. And I'm not saying that is with every woman. I'm saying the one who tames your ass without even knowing she's doing it. The woman who loves without boundaries and calls you on your bullshit but loves you when you don't even love yourself and are being an asshole. Those are the women men would walk through fire for. Do you know why she does it, Lance?"

"Why?"

"Because she knows that no matter what, in return, she will have respect, loyalty, faithfulness, and love." I nodded my head at his reply.

We were quiet for a few minutes, and I got up and went inside and grabbed a couple more beers, then brought them out, handing one over to my dad before sitting back down. It had been a while since my dad and I had hung out. We'd done it a lot as I was growing up, but of course it hadn't meant as much to me.

"You ever regret being strapped with a kid?" I asked, which I was sure had to be like the thousandth time since I was old enough to ask why I didn't have a mom around, and every time, he never failed to respond immediately.

"No."

"Oh, come on, old man. Not even one time?"

"No regrets. Now, did I have doubts about my ability to take care of you? Fuck yeah. Especially when you were first born and fighting off the drugs. You were tiny, and it scared the hell out of me. Like when you stayed awake for twenty-four hours and screamed the whole time. Or when you got older, and I put you in your crib for your nap, made sure you were asleep, then went to take a shower only to walk out of the bathroom to find you sitting in the middle of my bed covered in the baby powder you had grabbed from your room. But no matter what you did, you always had a smile on your face. Shakes was the first one who started calling you Devil because of it."

"I never knew that. Earliest I remember anyone calling me that, I was a teenager," I said, and my dad chuckled.

"Yeah, she was afraid the name would stick, so she yelled at any of us who called you that out loud." He chuckled and took a drink of his beer. "It stuck the day when you were fourteen and the sheriff brought you home after he caught you running between the houses in town with just your shirt on, carrying your damn pants."

"That was because old man Collier was chasing my ass with a kitchen knife!" I smiled, then laughed.

"That right there is why Shakes called you Devil," he said and pointed at me. "It's the same smile you always wore when you were up to no good. Hell, you still do when you've done something or are getting ready to do something. And Collier was chasing your ass because he walked in his house to find his eighteen-year-old daughter getting banged on his kitchen table."

"Not my fault the man came home for lunch that day." We both laughed because that was the exact thing I said when the sheriff questioned me.

"Damn, Collier moved his family a few months after that. The man had wanted to murder you, but Sheriff Lance reminded him that his daughter was the adult while you were a minor. Then the man ended up finding out she enjoyed teaching the younger boys because they were eager to please and would do whatever she asked."

"Hey, I had no complaint," I said, and my dad stood and shook his head.

"On that note, I think I'm going to head home." He pointed to the beer bottle he set on the little table between the chairs. "You got that, or you want me to go toss it?"

"Nah, I got it," I said, then added. "I saw and spoke to Bailey today," just as he stepped off the porch.

He turned around and faced me. "You don't say."

"You asked what had put the smile on my face when you first got here."

My dad nodded and then began to walk away before he replied over his shoulder, "Wondered if you were ever going to pull your head out of your ass, son."

I smiled, shook my head, grabbed the empty bottles off the table, and headed into the house without replying.

What was there to say? He was right.

Chapter Four

Bailey

"Are you sure you'll be okay by yourself? I could reschedule with Mackenzie if you need me to."

"Bailey, will you stop worrying? I will be fine. It's not like you'll be gone all day. Plus, it's not like I haven't been in the shop by myself before. I'll hear the bell when it rings." Mom huffed and turned back to rolling out the pie dough.

"I know, but if it gets busy or you start to feel bad, you call me." It would be the first time my mom would be left alone. Well, since her illness. I knew she would be okay. It was just going to take me a little time to let go. Since her diagnosis, it was as if my mother and I had switched roles.

"Yes, dear." I saw her lips twitch as she tried not to smile. Grinning, I walked to the back door. "Good luck, Bailey. You deserve something nice to happen to you."

I moved back toward her and wrapped my arms around her, hugging her. "Thanks, Mom. Love you."

"I love you too, honey. Now tell Mac she'd be a fool not hire you."

"You got it. I will be back as soon as I'm done." Mom went back to her crust, and I headed to the doctor's office.

When I reached Dr. Minton's office, I parked and walked in. The waiting area was empty and only Amedia, the receptionist, sat behind the counter.

"Hey, Bailey."

"Hi, Amedia. Is Mackenzie in? I'm supposed to meet with her."

"Yes. Dr. Minton's in with her last patient, so if you'll have a seat, I'll let her know you are here."

"Thank you." I turned and moved to the waiting area and took a seat. I didn't have to wait long before Dr. Minton walked out.

"Bailey, come on back to my office, and we'll talk." I followed her to the back, and once we reached her office, she waved to a chair in front of her desk, and I sat down. "So, you finally got your results? That's great. Now, when can you start?"

"Mom said you would be a fool not to hire me," I said, and started laughing.

"How is your mom doing at the bakery?"

"She is doing great, Mac. Me. I'm trying not to watch every move she makes and worry that she's doing too much. I think I'm getting on her nerves."

"Well, taking this job will help, Bay. She needs to get back into her routine."

"I know. She's been back less than a week. The first couple of days, she only worked a few hours. That was as long as it lasted. The last couple of days, she has stayed the entire time with me, baking, waiting on customers... everything. And I spend the day watching her. You might be right. Taking this job could be good for both of us." I chuckled. "Mom will probably dance around for finally getting me out of her space."

"It will be good for her. She needs to get back to her life, Bay, and you need to get on with yours."

"You're right, and that's what she said, too."

"So, can you start tomorrow?" I had to have had a shocked looked on my face because Mac burst out laughing. "Don't panic, I was just teasing. But seriously, though, when would you be able to start? Mabel wants to retire and spend time with her grandbabies. She's only still here because I told her once your results were back that you would take over."

I shook my head. "What were you going to tell her if I failed?"

Mac laughed. "I do not know. Now I don't need to worry about it since you passed."

"Okay, I guess if I'm going to be your new RN, I should pick up a few extra sets of scrubs. The ones I had from school are a little worn. Plus, who knows if they fit after working in the bakery with all the sampling." I stood, and so did Mackenzie.

"Please, you look great. At least you have curves, and they are in the right places." Mac waved her hand down her body. "Mine resembles a teenage boy's body with boobs."

I couldn't help it. I laughed. Mac was dainty and looked as if she should still be in high school, instead of a doctor running her own practice.

"Laugh. You will see. Some of the older patients who stayed with me after I bought out Dr. Davis when he retired call me the female Doogie Howser." I laughed harder at her expression. "Do you know who that is?" she asked and raised her eyebrows, waiting for my reply.

"Maybe."

"See? I had to ask who they were talking about. How was I to know it was a TV show from the late eighties about a teenage boy, no less, who was some type of medical phenomenon?"

"Mac, you are absolutely gorgeous. And you do not have the body of a teenage boy. I wish mine was as toned as yours."

"Yeah, and I wish I had some of your curves." Mac changed from ranting to chuckling, then continued, "We could sit here and bitch about what we don't like about our bodies, or we could say screw it and go to lunch instead. What do you think? Got time to have lunch with your soon-to-be employer before my afternoon appointments start?"

I thought of my mom at the bakery by herself and was ready to decline, but thought better of it. "Let me check in with Mom to make sure she's doing alright, and if she is, I am all for eating out with my new boss." I reached into my purse and pulled out my cell while Mac took off her white coat and hung it on the rack in the corner, then got her own purse out of a drawer in her desk. By the time she was ready, I had told my mom that I would see her after we finished eating and ended the call. When I looked at Mac, she was smiling. "What?"

"Wow, Claire really is tired of you mothering her. I could hear her over the phone."

"Yeah, she is. I think this job is going to be great, not only for me but for her, too. You were right. I need to get back to my life and let her get back to hers."

We headed out of Mac's office and discussed what all my job would entail. Mabel would crossover with me for a couple of weeks so I could get acquainted with my job duties. A week from Monday, instead of going to the bakery, it seemed I would be headed for a new career. When we got close to the reception area, voices could be heard. And as we turned the corner, I smiled at the two women who stood talking.

"Damn, Sami, you don't do anything half-assed, do you?" Sami looked over Carly's shoulder at Mac and me and shook her head and smiled at us. Carly noticed and turned to face us.

"Hey, Bailey," Sami said, and then picked up the papers Amedia laid on the counter for her.

"Hi, it seems like forever since I saw you two." I stepped forward and hugged each woman.

"God, I know. How's your mom doing?" Sami asked, and I gave her the spiel and brought her and Carly up to date with my mom and said that I would start work at Dr. Minton's office soon.

"Well, you'll get to see Sami often then, since my brother seems to have super sperm," Carly said, and Sami popped her on the shoulder, and that was when I realized they weren't there just for an annual exam.

"Oh my God, you're pregnant. Congrats!" Sami nodded, and I hugged her again.

"Yes, it's still sinking in, but I'm excited." I noticed when Sami spoke her hand went to her stomach.

"That is awesome news. Do you have to be somewhere else, or can you join Mac and I at the diner for lunch?"

"That sounds great. Not like I have a job to go to," Carly said and looked down at the leg she was shot in and then back up. "Convalescent leave sucks balls."

"Good grief, I swear you live to gripe," Sami said, rolled her eyes, and then continued. "Lunch sounds fantastic. Plus, the pharmacy is just down the street, and I can drop off the prescription for the prenatal vitamins and pick them up when we are done eating."

"You don't have any more appointments today?" Carly asked Mac.

"Sami was my last of the morning. I'm good till after lunch." We headed for the door leading outside after Mac answered.

"It was great you could squeeze me in. Thank you, because if I had to listen to Kane for one more day, I might've smothered him with a pillow." Sami chuckled and smiled. And no way could any of us have missed the love that showed in her eyes when she spoke of Speed.

I wanted what Sami and Carly had found. The difference between the women from the first time we all met was staggering. "Black Hawk men seem to fit you. You two make me envious."

"Please, like you couldn't have your own, Bailey." Sami popped Carly on the arm, and we stopped right before opening the door to the outside.

"What is wrong with you? You are getting even more outspoken, and you were already bad before," Sami chastised Carly.

"What did I miss?" Mac asked, and I groaned.

Loved these women almost immediately after meeting them. I had seen Sami and Carly around town the few times I had come home to visit my mom. When I moved back, I met Sami at the diner and then was introduced to Carly. Mac, I met through my mom since she was the one who found the knot in mom's breast on her yearly visit. I introduced her to the other two women, and the four of us had hit it off and became friends. And as friends, things get shared, so they knew my past with Lance. Sami and Carly would also know that Lance came by the bakery, which unfortunately meant they were going to be like dogs with a bone.

"Lance went to the bakery a couple days ago to pick up dessert for dinner at Sami's house. Nothing *that* important." Carly smiled at Mac, and then asked, "Or was it, Bay?" I rolled my eyes, and Sami laughed.

"Well, could it mean that 'operation we ignore each other' is over?" Mac asked, and Carly and Sami both raised their eyebrows.

"He came in. Bought dessert and left." I moved around Carly, who stopped in front of the door. I pushed opened the door, and we all stepped out onto the sidewalk and stopped in our tracks when we saw the four men who leaned against their bike seats at the curb.

"Hey, baby. What's the medical verdict?" Speed asked and opened his arms, and Sami walked into them.

"It is a baby. What else did you think she is having?" Carly looked at Speed, and his lips twitched as he looked over Sami's shoulder.

"Well, since I found out I was related to you, thought I better ask." Sami smacked Speed's chest. "What? She started it." Everyone laughed, and Crusher held open his arms.

"Come here, sugar, and give me a kiss before you and your brother throw down like five-year-olds on the sidewalk." Even seeing it with my own eyes, I stared as Carly walked right into Crusher's arms without one smartass remark.

Speed spoke low with Sami, and then leaned down and kissed her. Crusher pulled Carly tight against him and did the same. I felt like an interloper and turned to talk to Mac. I felt eyes on me and knew Lance watched me from where he was parked next to Coast.

"Holy hell, I think I might need one of those too," Mac leaned into me and whispered. I knew she was talking about the men, and I chuckled. They were impressive. I couldn't dispute that. Mac hadn't spent time a lot of time around the men, but with Sami and Carly with two of them, she would get used to them.

"If you come over here, I can help you out with that, Doc," Coast said, and I looked over to see him staring at Mac, whose face was tinged pink.

"I didn't mean... I meant. The hell with it. I will not explain," Mac stammered, and I stared at her. Since I had known her, not once had I seen her thrown off kilter and not the confident doctor.

"I knew what you meant, sweetheart," Coast answered, and then Mac rolled her eyes, but didn't reply. When I looked over at Lance, who had yet to speak one word, he smirked, then winked at me. I wondered if there was a woman alive who could stay mad at these men for any length of time. That included me. I never was mad at him; my feelings had just been badly hurt when he'd just stopped coming around.

The other men let the women up for air, and both their faces were flushed. Carly recovered first.

"If we are going to have lunch at the diner, we better go now, or Mac isn't going to have a chance to eat."

"We'll follow you over and have lunch with you," Crusher said.

"We are capable of eating on our own. Aren't you needed back at Black Hawk?" Carly asked, and I crossed my fingers that Crusher would say yes and they would head back. I needed to have small doses of being around Lance to make sure I built my immune back up. I didn't think I could take another go-round with him and keep my heart intact. Preservation was key for me.

"Jag and Flirt have it covered. Besides, Shakes and a couple of the ol' ladies are cleaning up the houses," Crusher said, and then held up his hand when Carly got ready to dispute. "I told them not to bother with ours, same as Speed told them not to bother with his. They said until you were one hundred percent, they would be by to help and with Sami, it was more that it excited them about having a baby around so she may never have to straighten or clean house again."

"Well, that answers a lot. Jag is a slob, so he is more than likely picking up before they get there. Flirt is probably putting away his toys," Carly said and laughed.

"What do you know about Flirt's toys?" Crusher looked down at Carly and asked while the other men went quiet. Mac looked at me, and I shrugged. I had an idea what she meant, but no way was I going to get involved.

Carly patted Crusher's chest. "Women talk."

"They do, huh? Including you?" Crusher lifted a brow in question and smirked.

The men groaned, and Lance finally spoke. "Carly doesn't need to talk. I've said it a hundred times. Close. Your. Windows!"

Speed and Coast laughed. Carly blushed, Crusher grinned, and Sami shook her head.

"I'm sure Mac and I don't want to know. So, let's go eat." I turned to head to my car with Mac behind me.

"I might want to know," Mac said as she caught up.

"Trust me, I've known those men most of my life. You don't want to know."

Mac laughed, and we got into my car, and I pulled out.

Chapter Five

Devil

When we walked into the diner, after a stop at the pharmacy, the women had two tables pushed together and were seated at one, chatting and laughing. Speed sat in one of the empty chairs and then pulled the one out beside him and signaled for Sami to sit beside him. Crusher did the same with Carly, which opened the seats beside Bailey and Mac. I took the vacated one next to Bailey, and I noticed as Coast sat down in the other, Mac discreetly tried to scoot her chair away to put distance between her and Coast.

"If you try to move any farther away, Doc, you'll be sitting in Carly's lap." Coast leaned back in his chair and placed his arm over the back of her chair, stopping the movement.

"I was giving you more room. You are kind of... um, big." Mac glared at Coast. I could tell by my brother's actions toward the woman he was interested. When I glanced over at the others, they were watching them too.

"Yeah, I am," Coast winked at her, then continued, "all over."

"Oh my God, seriously? Does that shit work for you?" Mackenzie seemed to be losing some of her shyness. We'd only seen her around town a few times, and when we did, we would speak to her, and she would acknowledge us, then hurry away.

"I don't know. Is it?" Coast asked her and smirked.

Mac ignored him and picked her menu up and opened it. I wanted to tell her it wouldn't deter him. Once Coast zoned in on something, he was relentless.

"I'll tell you what I think," he said and leaned over and placed his mouth close to her ear. I couldn't hear what he whispered, but by the blush that formed on her face, it must have been good. I'd give her an 'A' for effort because she never said anything in response or turned to look at him.

I chuckled at him when he sat back in his chair again with a smug look on his face until a shooting pain pierced my thigh.

"What the fuck did you pinch me for?" I looked down at Bailey, who was suddenly interested in her menu, too.

"I don't know what you're talking about," Bailey said, set the menu down, and grabbed the water glass and took a drink while I stared at her.

"You're going with that, huh?" She cut her eyes to me and nodded. "Okay." It was all I said, and like Coast, I placed my arm over the back of her chair. "I owe you one, but when I go to pay you back, it won't be on the thigh." Sami and Carly laughed and smiled when Bailey glared at them.

"You men had to be a handful growing up," Mac said as Thelma, the owner of the diner, walked up with a notepad in hand to take everyone's order.

"Hon, you have no idea. This bunch has been trouble since they started to shave." Thelma looked at each of us and grinned. "And it looks like a couple of you forgot how to do that." She looked at Crusher and then at me. I smiled and spread my hand, placing my jaw and chin between the gap of my thumb and fingers, and ran them over my chinstrap and soul patch.

"You get younger every time I see you, Thelma."

"Lance Cummings, don't you start." She pointed her pencil at me. "You are worse than that one," the hand with the pencil moved to Crusher, who laughed. "Hell, every one of you was born with a silver tongue. I don't know why it should shock me. I went to school with your dads. When all of you walk in here, I feel like I'm thrown back to high school." Bailey and the other women snickered.

"Thelma, if I hadn't been scared that Wayne would've killed me back then, I would have tried to steal you away from him," I said, and Thelma laughed.

"Bailey, I hope you straighten that one out. Carly and Sami seem to be doing a decent job with those two." If Thelma didn't watch, she was going to put mine or Coast's eye out with the damn pencil she moved around as she talked.

"Oh, we aren't... Ow!" Bailey yelled and looked at me while her hand moved down and rubbed the side of her butt.

"Don't say stuff you know nothing about." Bailey frowned at my words.

"What the heck are you talking about?"

"You'll find out soon enough. Now give Thelma your order. I'm hungry." Bailey rolled her eyes, and Thelma wrote what she wanted and then moved on to the next one, with Coast being the last to place his order.

"I'll turn these orders over to the cook and be back with your drinks." Thelma walked away, and Bailey started back in.

"Are you going to tell me what you meant?"

"Nope." I grinned when she turned and huffed as Thelma returned with our drinks. I always loved pushing Bailey's buttons.

"Sami, I heard you're selling your place in town," Thelma said as she walked around the table and sat everyone's drinks down.

"Yes, I actually think I might have a buyer." Sami took a drink of her soda just as one of the other waitresses brought out our food and Thelma set the orders down in front of each of us.

"That's great, Sami. It is a nice house. I was going to ask if you had plans to rent it out."

"Oh, Bailey, I might have if I'd known you wanted to rent it. Even Speed suggested renting it out, but I didn't want to have to deal with renters. Carly lived there a whole two weeks and hadn't even moved in all the way." Sami chuckled.

"I can't help it if I was a little busy with work and then laid up. You can blame Crusher for costing you a renter, not me." Carly huffed as if she was offended, but then smiled when Crusher leaned over and kissed the top of her head.

"Damn right, and I will take the blame for the loss of rent to have you with me, sugar." Crusher picked up his burger and started eating when the other women said, "Ahhh."

"Going to get back to work. If you need anything else just yell."

"Sure thing, Thelma," was said in unison by the group as Thelma started to walk away.

"And the next time you see my two lug-head sons, tell them it would be nice if they stopped in and saw their mother every once in a while." Thelma didn't wait for a response from any of us because we knew she was joking. I knew for a fact, Bull and Tank took turns visiting her throughout the week and the men made a conscious effort to at least have dinner with her twice a month. It had been that way since their dad passed away not long after they graduated high school. The two men were a couple of years older than me and the others. They joined Black Hawk shortly before we left for the military. I figured Thelma was the reason they stayed instead of joining the military themselves. However, they had shocked her when, after joining Black Hawk, they both registered at the trade school in town and received their mechanic's licenses. Each one worked at Soft Tails as bouncers, and on their off days, they filled in at the garage the club owned to cover so the few members who worked there could have time off. But since Sami had been off, Tank had been filling in for her, and left the garage for Bull to cover.

Everyone began to eat and carry on individual conversations. I wanted to laugh as I watched and heard Coast trying to get Mac to engage with him. She would answer his questions, but never turned to look at him.

"So, you're looking for a place to rent?" I picked up my burger and waited for Bailey to answer. When she didn't, I turned toward her and watched as she moved a french fry around in the ketchup on her plate. As I watched her teeth bite down on her plump lip and then her tongue followed and licked across the spot, my dick hardened. I studied her face, her brown eyes focused on the fry, the darker blond lashes, long and from the angle that I watched, they damn near touched against her cheeks. She was so beautiful.

Before I knew what I was doing, I reached over and ran the knuckles of my hand down her cheek. She blinked a couple times, then turned and focused on me.

"Where were you, Bay?" I whispered and watched as she glanced around the table, making sure no one was paying attention to us.

"I've gotten over thinking of James every day, but when I least expect it, he'll pop into my mind." I turned my hand over, and she leaned her cheek into it. Touching her, the warmth of her skin against mine was the final straw for me. She'd be mine if it took the rest of my life to get her.

"It probably had to do with being here."

"Yeah, he was so outgoing and always the life of the party." She lifted her face away, and I moved my arm and wrapped it around her, resting my hand on her shoulder and squeezed. Then, caught in the moment, I leaned over and placed a kiss on her temple.

I lifted away, and she looked at me, her eyes focused on mine, asking what she wouldn't. Someone's clearing of their throat broke that moment, and my eyes moved around the table to find that everyone was watching us.

"Hey, Bailey, sorry to interrupt, but I need to head back to the office. My afternoon appointments will be showing up. The sooner I start seeing them, the sooner I am out of there."

"No problem. I need to get back to the bakery, too. Got a special cake to bake." Bailey looked over at Sami, who was grinning.

"Oh my God, Ally's birthday day and cookout party. I totally forgot. I'll be shopping after I leave the office today and I know exactly what I'm getting her." Mac went to stand, and Coast helped with her chair.

"Mac, you don't have to bring Ally anything. I invited you because I thought it would be a nice way to meet some of the single men in the area," Sami said, and Coast smiled down at Mac.

"Got something to look forward to." Mac rolled her eyes at Coast's words.

Everyone stood, and the other men and I tossed some cash on the table to cover Thelma and the other waitress's tip, and I picked up the checks the waitress had set on the end of the table as she had walked by with the order for the table behind us. I fished mine out and then handed the others to Coast, and he did the same, then handed the last two over to Crusher and Speed.

"Where's my ticket?" Bailey asked and looked at the end of the table as if more tickets would appear.

"Yeah, I didn't get one either," Mac added.

"Your food is on my ticket," Coast said.

"And I got yours, Bay." I pushed the chairs in and started toward the register.

"I can pay for my lunch," Bay said as she followed behind me.

"Sure you can. Don't make a big deal out of this. I got it." As the cashier rang it up, I reached into my pocket, pulled out the cash I had shoved into it and paid for our food.

"That goes for me, too. I don't expect for you to pay for my food." I smiled inwardly at Mac's response. Coast was going to have his hands full. That was if Mac even let him get close enough.

"I'm not complaining about paying for your lunch, so why are you bitching about it?" I moved to the side just as Coast spoke and set his ticket and cash on the counter.

"Trust me, this is not remotely close to me bitching. This wasn't as if we were on a date." Mac huffed. It took everything in me not to laugh. Coast paid the check and even spoke to the cashier as though Mac wasn't even talking to him. Though I knew the brother heard it all. When he was done, and his change was put away, he turned and stepped out of the way before responding.

"No, sweetheart, trust me—when we are on a real date, you don't want to bitch at me—because I will take you into the closest restroom and spank your ass." Mac's mouth dropped open, and Coast didn't say anything else he just turned, opened the door and walked out.

"Well, that was interesting," Carly said as she smiled and stood beside Crusher at the counter.

"Yeah, it was. Shows he's a dick," Mac said, then looked at Bailey and continued, "I'll meet you at the car." Before Bailey could respond, Mac was out the door.

"Thanks for lunch. I better get her back to the office and my butt to the bakery." Bailey hugged Carly and Sami. The women spoke to each other while Speed paid.

"You two look good together," Crusher said low so the women wouldn't overhear.

"Thanks, Prez."

"Hell, I still can't get used to that. There have been a few times someone's yelled out 'Prez,' and I've looked to see

where my dad was before it hits me they are yelling at me."
Crusher chuckled.

"Probably because we are lax in calling you that. We need to make an effort doing it. You are our Prez, and we should show the respect that position holds."

"Thanks, Dev."

With our bills paid, everyone walked out. When I stepped out onto the sidewalk and looked up and down the street, I noticed on one side Mac stood beside Bailey's car and was focused on her phone while at the other end, Coast sat on his bike and stared at her.

Sami's car was parked in front of our bikes, and Bailey's car was further down the street. As Speed and Crusher started helping Sami and Carly in the car, I headed the opposite direction to walk Bailey to hers.

"Everything okay with you, Bay?"

"Yeah, why?"

"Well, you were at the doctor."

"Oh, I was talking with Mac. I start work there a week from Monday."

"Fuck, Bay, that is awesome. Congrats. Proud of you. You're finally getting to do what you always wanted to." We reached the car, and she hit her key fob and the doors unlocked. Mac got in the passenger side and closed the door as I walked to the driver's side with Bailey.

"A little later than I planned, but that's okay." Bailey smiled and reached for the handle on the door.

"A lot of things are happening later than were planned." Bailey turned and frowned at me, and I stepped into her personal space. My hands went to the sides of her face and into her hair. I tilted her head up, and I lowered until my mouth took hers. The gasp from her parted her lips, which was enough to allow for my tongue to enter. Fuck going slow with her. It was long overdue to take what had always been mine.

As I devoured her on the street I heard "Get a room!" and a few "About time!" yelled, but the sounds were muffled. Only the woman and her taste were important to me. Bailey stiffened at first, but then relaxed and melted into me. One of her hands was still on the car door handle and the other was now braced on the side of the car as she used it to keep her balance.

I took one more swipe of the inside of her mouth and pulled back, planted a light kiss on her lips and then kissed her forehead before I released her and stepped away.

Bailey's eyes were clouded. Her face wore a look of confusion as she blinked and looked up at me.

"Why did you do that?" I looked down at her and smiled.

"Just my way of letting you know I'm coming for you. See you later, Bay." I turned and walked to my bike. When I reached it, I mounted, and my brothers said not one word. The smiles that were spread across their faces were all that was needed.

Chapter Six

Bailey

"You want to talk about what's bothering you, honey?" I closed the lid on the cake box. I knew my mom was worried. Yesterday, I had entered the bakery and went straight to the back with only a 'hey' to my mom. She tried a dozen times to get me to tell what was bothering me until finally she just gave up.

After we closed the shop and headed home, it was no different. We cooked dinner in silence and then watched TV with minimal conversation before I finally just said goodnight and went to bed. Sleep was hard to find, and when it came, Lance filled my dreams. I woke up a hot, sweaty mess that had nothing to do with nightmares, which I should have been thankful, but I wasn't. Instead, I was mad at my body for defying me. Even now, if I thought of the kiss, my heartbeat picked up, and my stomach felt as if butterflies filled it.

The shower I'd taken this morning, well, it had released a small amount of tension, only after I sat on the bench, spread my legs, and turned the vibrator on that I had snagged out of my nightstand. My clit pulsed and hardened as I moved the vibrator back and forth, teasing myself. I closed my eyes and thought of Lance: his touch, his lips on mine, then his descent down my body. I'd tweaked and pulled at my nipples as I imagined he sucked and licked them until they were peaked. As he reached my pussy, his tongue pressed on my clit, then moved to breach me, tonguing me to the brink before he stopped. I'd seen him behind my closed eyes as if he stood in the shower stall with me.

He pumped his cock, then he positioned me with my hands on the bench and my ass in the air as he entered me with one thrust of his hips. He pounded into me until we both climaxed. When I came down from my orgasm and opened my eyes, I was leaning against the wall, my vibrator buzzing in my hand. I was surprised my mom wasn't beating on the door because when my orgasm had hit, "Lance" was torn from my throat.

"Bailey, are you okay? Your face is flushed." The worry in my mom's voice made me realize how unfair I was to her. After everything she'd been through, she didn't deserve my crazy.

"He kissed me," I blurted out as I looked up at her from across the table.

"He who, Bailey? You haven't been the same since you came back yesterday from Mac's office and lunch. Did something happen during lunch? Did you not get the job?"

I pinched my nose between my finger and thumb, took a deep breath, and let it out slowly. When I dropped my hand away from my face, I looked into my mom's eyes.

"Lance," was all I said, and she nodded, then a smile started to spread. "I'm glad you find this amusing."

"Well, I should have known. You used to act the same way when you two were together."

"I most certainly did not do that."

"Bailey, how do you think I knew you were doing more than kissing Lance?"

"Because I asked you to take me to the doctor so I could get on birth control."

"I had already had an appointment made for you to see the doctor. That was why we got in so quick. I knew because at first, you would come home after being with him and tell me what the two of you did, in detail. Then one day you came home, and nothing from you other than you had fun. Later, I would catch you daydreaming, and you would smile to yourself. It had been that way for me with your dad, Bailey. I imagine it's like that for most young girls. For me, I knew that day, I was getting to watch my young daughter fall in love for the first time." When I didn't respond, she continued, "I guess if he kissed you, at some point yesterday you must have run into him?"

I nodded and shared with my mom everything from my talk with Mackenzie to Sami being pregnant, and then moved on to Lance. My mom listened without interruption as I went on and on. When I told her about the kiss and what Lance had said before he walked away and left me standing there, she was fanning herself.

That small gesture made me laugh. And sharing the events, getting them out in the open and off my chest, did wonders for me.

"Wow, that is just... I don't know what to say other than he has grown up into a helluva man." My mom kept fanning herself and grinning.

"I'm your daughter, and you're impressed with the man who kind of threatened me!"

"Pfft! Honey, that was not threatening. That, my dear, was a man going for what he wants. And it seems to be you."

"No, I refuse to deal with this. I was only hurt the first time around. I'm afraid if I allow a second and it ends... it could break me." The last part I whispered, and Mom moved around the counter and put her arms around me.

"Honey, do you think Lance set out in the beginning to hurt you?"

"No, I don't want to believe he could ever be cruel like that." I laid my head on my mom's shoulder and, like she did a hundred times with me, she moved a hand over the back of my head. It comforted me when I was young, and it had the same effect on me now.

"When you and Lance started dating, your daddy worried. At first, it was because those boys had reputations that followed them all over town. But the longer you two were together, his worry changed. Like me, he saw the two of you becoming closer, getting attached to one another. And he saw how Lance looked at you when he thought no one was watching, and it scared your dad." I lifted my head and moved out of her arms.

"Why?"

"Because he saw the boy loved you. And he knew you loved him. It scared him when Lance left for Basic Training, then returned after he finished. He thought Lance would take you with him when he left again. He knew you would go with him if he asked. And you were so young, both of you were."

"Well, he worried about nothing."

"I guess what I'm trying to say, Bailey. You might have been young, but the love you two shared was more than what some older couples share. That doesn't just go away. I know I've asked you before if you were still in love with him. But what I'm going to ask this time is the love you hold for him worth a second chance? Or are you going to let a little hurt leave you with a lifetime of regret?"

"I don't know. I wish I did."

"Do you think if I had known I would lose your dad before he turned forty-five, I wouldn't have married him? And do you think I regret having James because he died way too early in his life?"

"No, you couldn't have known any of that was going to happen. You don't regret it, do you, Mom?

"No. I would do it all again, even knowing what was going to happen. Because I can't imagine having even one day without your dad or James in it." I felt the tears at the corner of my eyes ready to overflow when my mom finished.

"You are one smart woman, Mom." I hugged her.

"I know. It is such a burden." My mom always knew how to lighten up a mood.

"What do you say we go to a birthday party and cookout?"

"I would say 'yes.'"

I taped the lid of the box so it would stay closed. We didn't need to check the front shop because we had already closed for the day and locked up. I grabbed the large cake, and my mom opened the back door, then locked it. After we had situated the cake to where it wouldn't bounce around, we got in the car, and I pulled out and headed to Black Hawk.

"Did I mention that before your dad and I got together, I dated Michael Browning?"

"You went out with Romeo, Flirt's dad? Oh, my God, no you did not." My mom seemed to be full of surprises today.

"Yep, then he left for the military, and I got with your dad, and that was that."

"You never know, Mom. He'll be at the cookout," I teased.

"Yeah, because most men would want a woman with hair that was just coming back and no breasts." Mom touched the bandana she had on her head and looked down at the loose-fitted blouse she wore.

"Stop that. You have battle scars, but you won the war. I don't want to hear you talk like that about yourself. You are still a beautiful woman, inside and out."

The rest of the drive to Black Hawk was quiet. I stayed focused on the road while Mom looked out the passenger window. When I turned off the road and the gate came into view, my mom broke the silence.

"Bailey, you have always been the best daughter a woman could have. I love you, honey."

"I love you too, Mom. Now let's go have some fun, like the single, eligible women we are!" I laughed, and so did my mom.

We were still laughing when I stopped for the man at the gate.

Chapter Seven

Devil

The others and I were in the office in the clubhouse having a meeting when Crusher's cell rang. While I sat listening to the one-sided conversation, I tilted my chair back on two legs and leaned my head against the wall. Last night had left me restless and tired. The text I received from my mother's acquaintance, code for pimp/drug dealer, hadn't helped either. It had only added to the restlessness because I couldn't shut my brain down. Thoughts of how I was going to handle Bailey along with the 'how the fuck did the dude get my damn number' and 'why I would be interested in anything that belongs to the woman who gave birth to me,' kept me chasing sleep. When I finally crashed, the sun was beginning to rise. I'd woken to Flirt banging on the door to tell me we were going to have a meeting before the cookout started. I got up, showered, and headed to the clubhouse. The only thing I had settled in my head was today I was going to tell Bailey everything since I planned to get her back. She deserved to know, and we needed to start with a clean slate. When Crusher said goodbye, I placed the chair back down on all fours so we could get back to our meeting.

"Well, that was Creed." Crusher sat his phone down and continued, "He wanted to set up a pickup place and time. They still have a few issues they need to clean up, but with some developing new intel, Jas needs to be with them. He also said the other club may already know where she is or at the very least an idea of it, so we need to keep our eyes out for anyone or anything out of the ordinary in the area. I'll inform the club tomorrow at Church."

"Ops got a particular timeframe they want to do this?" Jag asked, and the rest of us waited for Crusher to answer.

"As soon as we can arrange it. He didn't go into everything, but he said yesterday wasn't soon enough. The only thing he added was things were getting ready to get handled, and he wanted everyone in his club close because he was tired and over the psycho bitch and her puppets. And then there was a woman's voice yelling in the background something about 'hell called and needed the motherfuckers back.'" Crusher chuckled.

"Damn, we have got to make sure their women never get near ours," Speed said, and we all laughed at the expression on his and Crusher's faces.

"No shit, Carly is bad enough. The woman doesn't need anyone giving her more ideas." Crusher leaned forward and placed his elbows on his desk. "So, I guess we need to decide who and when, so I can let Shakes and Dare know their house guest is moving on."

"Shakes has gotten attached to that girl. Jas has done well there too. Dare took to her right off because of her toughness. Hope the Ops and her momma don't get upset," Flirt said.

"Shit, Dare has had that girl out firing weapons, and she is spot fuckin' on with any gun given to her," I chuckled, then continued. "Plus, he's been teaching her how to ride. He still had one of those old bikes we had ridden around the property before we were old enough to get our licenses. It hadn't run when he dug it out, but he took it and Jas to the garage. Those two worked on that bike for weeks before they got it running. I don't think her momma is going to be upset. I think she's going to be impressed. Shady let a young girl come here, but she gets a young woman back. A tough damn young woman at that." My brothers nodded in agreement with me.

"Still need to figure out when and who," Coast reminded us.

"If they could meet us in San José, I would go. Got a text last night from some asshole that knows my mother." When my brothers looked at me, I continued, "It would seem that's where she's living now. Couple day's ride for us, but I could see what the prick has that is so important to text me and then check to see what they arrested the bitch for this time. The more I think about the text, it's more likely she needs fucking bail money and hopes I give a shit enough to pay it."

"Count me in. I'll go to represent the club as VP. That way, you can stay back with Carly, Prez. Then I can be there if Dev goes off and ends up needing legal representation." I shook my head at Jag.

"Really? If I were going to do anything to go to jail, it would be for more than that woman."

"I can go too, for backup," Coast added.

"Let's send Brax instead. We planned to make him a full member at Church tomorrow. He can drive the truck with Jas and her things while Devil and Jag ride as backup. If that group has someone in the area watching us, sending an enforcer will draw attention. They will assume we are moving something. Jas can hunker down in the truck when you guys pull out. Once you clear no one is following, the trip should be uneventful. If someone is, then you call back, and we can head in your direction and put the bastards in the middle. Anyone see a problem with that?" Crusher looked at each of us and waited. Everyone shook their heads.

"I know everyone knows Brax's story about how he ended up coming to Black Hawk with me. He also did well taking out that rogue bastard from Haven. When Brax was on my SEAL team, we labeled him Ghost. I'd like to suggest that as his club name too." Flirt smiled and added, "Fucker is big, but you've seen him move. He fits the statement 'silent but deadly.' So, if you find out someone is following you, no better man to have with you."

"Well, if we are all in agreement. Dev, Jag, and Brax will meet up with the Ops. And I guess Ghost it is for Brax's club name. Jag, Devil, when do you want to pull out? The Ops wanted it to happen fast. Anyone got anything going on that would keep them from leaving Monday? Two days to get to San José and you could meet up with the Ops on Wednesday."

"Works for me. Then I can swing by to see what is up with my mom and we can head back after." I looked toward Jag, and he agreed.

"Okay, let me call Creed back and see if this all works for them." Crusher picked up his cell while we waited. The call didn't take long, and when he hung up, he was chuckling. "I do not envy Creed. How he can talk on the phone with those women in the background is beyond me. Anyway, they can do it. Fork, Cajun, who is one of Jas's stepdads, and a couple of women will make the meet. I'll speak to Brax at the cookout, make sure he is good to go. So, anything else we need to handle before we break and head outside to have some fun?"

"Nah. Everything is set up and ready. A few of the men have the grills going and coolers filled. The women have everything else covered," Speed said and then looked at each of us.

I noticed since we'd been in the meeting; he had been quieter than usual and for Speed that was something because the man said few words in the first place. Speed stood and slid his hand into the pocket of his jeans. When he pulled it out, his hand held a little square box. Speed moved, so he faced us all, and with his other hand, he lifted the lid.

"Had this for a couple of weeks. Been waiting for the perfect time. Wanted to give you all an advance notice, so you don't say some rude shit thinking you're all funny and make Sami cry. It's my daughter's birthday. I just found out I'm going to be a dad again, and I want my ol' lady to accept this and make it all legal. So, don't make me beat anyone's ass today."

"Congrats, brother!" I was the first one out of my chair to congratulate him.

"Your ass is trying to make me look bad," Crusher said and hugged Speed. After the man hugs and pats on the back had been done, we started to walk out of the office.

"Wild Bill should be happy that you're making an honest woman out of his little girl. How'd he take the news of the baby?" I asked and opened the office door.

"I didn't get a chance to tell him last night since he and Keg pulled in late. Before Sami could broach the subject this morning, he figured it out on his own when she ate, then took off in a run for the bathroom. Evidently, morning sickness has kicked in." When I looked over at Speed, his lip was curled.

"Was it that bad?" I asked and couldn't hold back the laughter at his expression and neither could the others.

"Fuck off. I'd like to see you guys deal with watching your woman hugging the toilet like it's her best friend, and you know she's having to do it because she's carrying your kid. I got a cold cloth and put it on her neck while I held her hair back. Then I stood there and wondered where all of it was coming from because her ass hadn't eaten that much at breakfast."

"Goddammit, Speed. There is sharing, brother, but hell..." Flirt walked out, shaking his head. "I could have done without the visual." We headed down the hall behind him toward the kitchen in the back of the clubhouse.

"You didn't say if Wild Bill was happy or not?" Jag asked.

"He was happy, but mentioned if we had plans to get married, then Keg had a smartass remark, and before I could say anything, Sami jumped down both their throats. After she told them it was our business if we married or not, and to butt out, she then burst into tears and shouted that I hadn't even asked her so how could we get married? I pushed my chair back and stood to go to her, and she pointed at me with one hand while she wiped her tears away with the other and yell that it was my fault she was acting like a crazy person. Then she stormed out of the kitchen. Shit, Wild Bill looked at me, said welcome to the hormonal pregnant woman experience, and got up to go get cleaned up. As he passed by me leaving the kitchen, he warned me I might want to hide any sharp objects until after the baby was born. Oh, and mind you, the 360 personality changes in Sami happened in less than three minutes."

"Well, guess I won't be getting Carly pregnant anytime soon," Crusher said as we stepped out the back door and into mayhem. The celebration of Ally's party was underway as kids ran around shooting each other with water guns. Sami had a few of the brothers helping her set up some games for the kids, who were running around the yard shooting water guns at each other.

"Hey, kid!" We turned when we heard Carly's voice in time to see one of the little boys stop and look back at her.

Coast groaned, "Shit, I hope parents aren't going to be calling me," just as Carly pulled the biggest damn water gun I had seen from behind her back. The poor kid never had a chance as she let loose on him.

"I can actually see Carly as one of those animals that eat their young," Coast said, and Crusher slapped him on the back.

"Coast, she hears you say that she might shoot your ass and not with a water gun. And I will let her," Crusher said, and then he headed toward Carly while Speed headed toward Sami.

"I could picture her as a Praying Mantis. They bite the head off the male after they mate," Jag said as he looked around the yard. When no one said anything, he looked back to me, Coast, and Flirt as we stood there staring at him. "What? I know other shit besides the law, dickheads."

"Yeah, it's the random shit that worries us," I said as I watched Bailey's car pull into the open area off to the side that was used for extra parking. "Going to help Bailey," I added and walked away in her direction.

I did not know when I was going to explain everything to Bailey, but as I watched her get out of the car, and the thought of leaving in two days came to mind, settled it. I didn't want to leave things hanging between us until I got back.

Bailey got out of the driver's side, then opened the back door and bent inside. I admired the way the jeans hugged her ass as I made my way to her. When I reached her, I stepped up behind her and ran both my hands over her ass and squeezed.

"Hey, baby. You need help with anything?" Caught off guard, she rose from the car and bumped her head.

"Dammit, Lance!" she yelled as she spun around to face me. I grabbed her hips to steady her, then bent and kissed the top of her head. I let her go as the passenger side door opened and her mom got out.

"You after my daughter again?"

"Mom!"

"Sure am. Going to catch her too. You going to have a problem with that?"

"Oh, my God, Lance!"

"I don't imagine if I did, it would do any good. Would it? Now bring your handsome self over here and give me a hug."

I chuckled and walked around the car to meet Claire at the back. When I reached her, I wrapped her in my arms and hugged her.

"Don't hurt her this time." I'd barely heard the words Claire said because she spoke so low.

"No plans to do that. She's mine, always has been," I replied as low as Claire had, and before I let her go, I kissed the top of her head like I had done to Bailey.

"If you two are done acting like I'm not standing three feet away, I need help getting this cake out of the backseat."

"No one has forgotten you're here. Relax. It's not every day a woman gets to be held in the arms of such a hot young man."

"Mom, what has gotten into you?" I chuckled at the women's banter, and when Bailey cut her eyes toward me, I winked at her.

"Must be the fresh air," Claire said, and Bailey shook her head and rolled her eyes.

"Then try not to breathe too deep," Bailey replied, and I couldn't hold in the laughter. Evidently, the women couldn't either as they both joined in.

"Claire? Glad to see you out." Bailey grinned at her mom when Romeo, Flirt's dad, walked up and spoke.

"Michael, it's good to be out. How have you been?" Romeo nodded at me, told Bailey hi, and then put his arm around Claire's shoulders.

"I could ask you the same thing, but you seem to be doing really well. I'm glad, was worried about you for a bit. Come on, let's get you a drink and some food. You can sit with me and the others, and we will catch up." Before Bailey and I could say anything, Romeo whisked Claire off toward where the other dads sat.

"Well, well," Bailey said, and I looked at her.

"Why are you grinning?"

"Did you know those two dated before my mom met my dad?"

"No shit?" I looked at Bailey, and she chuckled.

"Yeah, that was pretty much my first response." Bailey grabbed a bag out of the floorboard in the back, then moved out of the way so I could reach the cake.

"Damn, that is a big ass cake." I bent and slid the box to the edge so I could get a good grip on it.

"Well, I wanted there to be enough."

"No worries there, Bay. How did you get this to your car? Thing probably weighs thirty pounds."

"Stop whining. It doesn't weigh that much. Now be careful. I got it in the car and here without damaging it. You only have to get it to a picnic table." Bailey shut the doors after I had the cake held in my arms. When we reached the picnic table decorated for Ally's party, I sat the box down in the middle.

"Where is Sami putting Ally's presents?" I pointed to the table set off to the side and out of the way. "Well, she is going to be one happy little girl. You know you men are spoiling her, right? No one will ever measure up when she gets older."

I turned toward Bailey and then followed where she looked.

"Hell, if Tank falls, he will crush one of those kids or several." Tank stood blindfolded under a branch that had a motorcycle piñata hanging down from it while his brother, Bull, helped Ally turn Tank in circles.

"I would be more worried when he swings the stick. Why men don't use the sense God gave them leaves me baffled at times."

"Hope you don't expect me to answer that?" I said and wrapped my arms around her waist from behind and pulled her against me. Bailey stiffened at first, then I felt her slowly relax against me. She turned her head to the side and up to look at me.

"What is this, Lance? Why suddenly the change? One day you're in the bakery, and the next you're kissing me and telling me you are coming after me. Now, this."

"I know we need to talk and that I owe you an explanation, or at least some answers. But can we enjoy the party before we dive into everything?"

"Fine, but don't think you're going to force me into anything."

"Bet I could." I spun her, then leaned my head enough to capture her lips with mine. The longer we stood there, the more I wanted to swing her up into my arms and carry her to my house. I broke the kiss and stepped back.

"You've got the best mouth," she said as she opened her eyes and looked up at me. "But that isn't going to get you your way."

I leaned closer and lowered my voice so only she would hear me, "I'm pretty sure it can if I lay you down and throw your legs over my shoulder and use it on your pussy till you're screaming my name and begging for my cock. You remember, like you used to do." When I stood up straight and looked at her, her eyes were wide, and I didn't miss the shiver of her body as I spoke to her.

"Oh, my God, I can't believe you said that. We are at a party and a children's party at that." I started laughing, and she glared at me. "How can you find this funny?"

"Come on, let's go join the others. We wouldn't want to miss any of the fun because if you thought the piñata was a potential hazard with men. You're going to love pin the muffler on the bike." I grabbed her hand and started walking us toward the tables where the others sat.

"Uh, pin the muffler?"

"Please, it was the cleanest version of the game they came up with." Bailey laughed and was still laughing when we sat down.

Chapter Eight

Bailey

It turned out to be one of the best days I've had in a long time. And it was nice to watch my mom enjoying herself, too.

"You did a terrific job on the cake, Bay?" Devil sat next to me with two plates with cake on them.

"Thanks, I worked on it most of the day yesterday and finished it up this morning."

"Ally was really surprised when Sami lifted the lid, and she saw it was a motorcycle. You even had it detailed with the Black Hawk patch on the gas tank."

"Sami gave me a picture of the one on the side of Speed's tank. It was kind of fun decorating the cake. When I first told Sami I would try to make it, I was worried."

"Well, you did great, Bay. Have you enjoyed yourself today?"

"Yes, I have. This has been an awesome day. I got to watch a good friend accept the proposal from the man she loves. I made a little girl I adore, happy with a cake. Then I got to watch the same little girl break down in tears when you men rolled that motorcycle around the building."

"Yeah, but I really thought Sami was going to kill us until Speed rushed to tell her it is electric powered for now." Lance chuckled and took the last bite of his cake.

"No way Sami could have stayed mad once she heard how you all built that bike with parts from Speed's dad's bike. I don't think any woman here didn't have tears in their eyes. Damn, I know I did."

"That's why the other day, Jag and Flirt stayed here when we came to town. We had to keep Sami and Carly from coming home so they could put the finishing touches on it and get it out of the garage and moved. Stroker put it in his shed until today."

"I thought he was going to rebuild Cutter's bike for himself?" I sat my fork down and turned on the bench toward Lance.

"He was, but then he said he wouldn't want to ride it and it would just sit in the garage. So, when Ally showed her interest in everything to do with bikes, we figured, what the hell? I mean, we build bikes. Why couldn't we build one and scale it down to fit her size? We used what we could off Cutter's, kept the parts from his that couldn't be sized down and Speed put those away for later when Ally is big enough to handle a real motorcycle."

"Well, it was the perfect gift for her, and the training wheels were too cute. I want to know who put the pink striping on it?" I giggled at the look on Lance's face.

"It wasn't me. I voted for flames on the tank. Coast did all the pink."

"Coast looked disappointed when Mac didn't get to stay." Lance shifted to straddle the bench facing me.

"Yeah, I think he was looking forward to spending time with her. Too bad she got called away no sooner than she got out of her car."

"She will be disappointed at what she missed, but then again, she left to bring a little person into the world."

"Are you looking forward to starting work at her practice?"

I smiled. "Yes. I was worried at first because of leaving my mom alone at the bakery so soon. But today helped to ease that worry." I looked over at the table where my mom sat with Romeo and the other dads. She was laughing at something one of them said. "Watching her have fun for the first time in a long while, especially when in the beginning, we didn't know if she would make it through everything, made for an outstanding day."

"I'm sorry, Bay, for not being there," Lance said, and all I could do was nod. He reached out and pushed a piece of hair that had escaped my ponytail away from my face. Lance studied my face and his brows creased. Then he stood.

"Something wrong?" I looked up at him, and he held his hand out for me to take.

"It's time."

"Time?"

"Yeah, it's time for you to get an explanation. Let's go down by the lake." I nodded and took his hand and stood.

"I need to check on my mom first. Make sure she is good to wait for me to get back." Lance nodded, and we walked to the table my mom sat at.

"Mom, Lance and I are going to walk down to the lake. Are you good until I get back or if not—" I didn't get to finish before Romeo cut me off.

"You kids go ahead. I'll take Claire home when she gets tired or is ready to leave. We," Romeo waved his hand at the other men at the table, which included Sami's dad and brother, "are going down to Soft Tails later so I can drop her off then." Romeo turned to my mom, who sat beside him. "You good riding on the back of my bike? If not, it isn't a problem, I will take you in my truck."

"I haven't ridden on the back of a bike in years. It should be fun. Go ahead, Bailey. I'll be fine and that way you don't have to hurry or rush home. Enjoy yourself for a change," she said and smiled at me.

"Are you sure?"

"Positive." My stomach might have rolled with Lance's 'it's time' because I didn't know what he was going to say or if I was ready to hear it. But my mom, enjoying herself, had me smiling back at her.

"Okay, I won't be too late." Lance and I started to walk away.

"You're an adult, Bailey. You can stay out as long as you want. Just text if you aren't coming home!" my mother yelled, and the men at the table chuckled. Lance squeezed my hand, and I didn't even answer or turn around. I waved over my head and kept on walking. We passed the others as they watched Ally ride her bike. We didn't stop, we only waved and the expressions on their faces varied from uncertainty to worry to knowledge. None made me feel any better.

Lance shook out the blanket we'd grabbed from his house and laid it down on the ground. He sat and then held out his hand, and when I placed mine in his, he helped me lower to the blanket. Once I was seated, he moved and positioned himself behind me and leaned against the tree. When he wrapped his arms around me and pulled me back against his chest, I felt seventeen again. I realized then I missed this, the closeness to him that had been built when we were younger. Hell, I plain missed him.

Neither of us had spoken on the way to the lake nor in the time since we arrived. Lance wanted to talk with me, and I guess he would when he was ready. While I waited, I looked out across the water and listened to the sounds of nature around us. Lance and I had done exactly this on more than one occasion that it felt familiar, yet somehow not.

"You warm enough, Bay?" Lance asked as he bent forward and placed his chin on my shoulder.

"Yes, I'm fine. The breeze actually feels nice. Lance?"

"Yeah?"

"What's this about? Why did you bring me here to talk?" I couldn't hold out any longer. The need to know what was going on with him won out. He leaned back against the tree again and pulled me even closer as I literally laid against his chest, his arms wrapped around me with his hands resting on my stomach. I felt his chest rise and fall against my back. When he sighed, I tried to turn around to face him, but his arms tightened, stopping me.

"Don't, Bailey. Let me talk and when I'm done, then if you want to look at me, you can. Okay?"

"Why wouldn't I want to look at you?"

"Bailey," he said and sighed again.

"Fine, but now you have me a little scared of what you're going to say."

"Christ."

"He's not here, so get on with it." I knew I was bitchy, and I couldn't bring myself to care. I really was getting nervous about what he wanted to say. And then, he took a deep breath and started, and the nervousness left, replaced by every emotion possible until there was none left to feel.

"Some you probably heard, but I'm going to start from when I left, anyway. Basic Training was easy mostly, and AIT for my MOS came naturally to me. Being trained as a medic made me happy. I had every intention of coming home on leave then, but as I graduated, the situation started heating up in the Middle East and everyone was needed. My unit shipped out to the desert after I was at my duty station for a month. I was geared up and ready to fight for my country. I had the knowledge and the training, but as I look back now, being green doesn't even touch what I was when we arrived and saw the devastation that had already happened there. Anyway, I worked through all of that at about the six-month mark. Not going to go into it, but I witnessed enough death and saw enough of my brothers wounded to harden me. Well, at least I thought that at the time.

"My unit was out on patrol when the ground shook around us. After we had checked in, the call came to my sergeant that a group of Marines had been hit in the vicinity where we were patrolling. The majority were wounded, and they had some fatalities too, which included the corpsman that was with them. It wasn't or isn't uncommon for the different branches of services to help each other. So, after we got the coordinates, my unit started making our way to the Marines. When we reached them, everyone started pitching in with the wounded, doing anything they could until I and the other medic with me could get to each one."

"Parameters were set up so we could watch the area in case another attack was to happen. I know it sounds strange, but that was unlikely to take place because it had been a typical hit and run."

"What's that?" I hated to interrupt him because I was afraid he would stop talking and I wanted to hear what he had experienced. It gave me a small glance into what he'd been through and even some of what my brother could have endured while there.

"When there isn't enough of the enemy present to have a full out attack, they make a quick hit to take out as many as possible, then they flee just as fast, so they don't get caught. The unit we were helping got hit by IEDs, improvised explosive devices, which were launched, and the insurgents luckily didn't stick around to finish the job, which means there was probably not enough of them to fight the remaining soldiers or they simply fired what they had. Sometimes we found no logical explanation for their actions. That is when we chalked it up to them wanting to kill any of us. Didn't matter the number, just so there were some.

"Anyway, I had kneeled beside a corporal who was bleeding out. With so many men injured, we evaluated the most critical down to the ones who could wait. While I was checking the corporal, I heard a deep voice say Devil, and I froze for a second, then turned and looked into the face of your brother."

"James," I said in a whisper. My God, he had been with my brother when he died. "You were there?" I sat up quickly, not giving Lance a chance to hold me in place and turned and straddled his lap. His head was back against the tree, and his eyes were closed. I placed a hand on each of his cheeks and held his face. When he opened his eyes, the pain was visible. "Tell me, please. Finish telling me."

"I won't tell you anything about his injuries other than he was messed up. James died because I let him die."

I gasped at his words but still held his face between my hands, though his eyes were focused over my shoulder. I knew he saw more than the lake.

"James's squad had been the first to reach the area, and out of them, he and one other soldier were alive. I stopped the bleeding on the corporal and moved to James, but he argued with me to save a soldier in his squad because the guy had two small kids he needed to go home to. Fuck, he even argued while I worked to stabilize him enough to either get airlifted out in one of the two choppers in route or at the very least to stay alive long enough to last the ride into the compound so the docs could get to work. I yelled at him when he said he wasn't going to make it.

"The choppers were five minutes out. They had been dispatched from another base three kilometers south. The deuce and a half, along with the other vehicles from the bases close by, wouldn't be there for ten to fifteen minutes."

It broke my heart into pieces as I listened to Lance. The pain was clear not only in his eyes but in his face and voice.

"Lance—" I was going to tell him to stop. He'd been through so much more than I would ever know about, but he cut me off.

"I need to finish, Bailey. I've carried it too long and let it eat at me," he said, and I nodded. "As I worked on him, he just kept saying over and over to let him go."

"Let me go, Dev."
"You're going to be okay, James. I can stop the bleeding."

"Look at me. I'm messed up, man."

"You're going home, James. We'll get you back, and the docs will fix you up. You, me, and the others have a lot of riding to do together. Black Hawk needs a new prospect."

"You and I know I'm never riding again, even if I live. But I'm not, Dev. I'm torn up inside. I can feel it. Let me go. Walk away, and help PVT Marks get back home. Tell my family I love them and, Lance, take care of Bailey, man."

"Come on, you don't want to go, James. I can hear the choppers. I'll make sure you get on the first one."

"Please, Dev, save Marks."

"I'll check on him, but your ass is on one of those birds. You hear me? We're brothers, and we always have each other's back, always."

"Sure, Dev. Go check on him, okay?"

"Yeah, but not until you promise to hold on. Don't give up."

"I promise. I'm not going anywhere."

"I went to PVT Marks. The other medic had the tourniquets on his legs, and he was as stable as he was going to get in the field. Someone yelled that the first chopper was on the ground. They landed in an open area close to where we were. I rushed to James so I could get him on that first one like I promised, but I knew before I even reached him, he wasn't going to make it. He got me to walk away. When I reached him, he..." Lance's eyes came back to mine. "He had undone a tourniquet I placed on him. With the blood loss he had sustained before we had reached him, that two minutes was all he needed. He'd already lost consciousness, and I reapplied pressure but, I was too late. I asked him 'why' even though I knew he couldn't hear me. As they reached us with the stretcher, he took a deep breath and went into cardiac arrest. Even the epinephrine and CPR couldn't bring back the beat to his heart."

"Oh, Lance, you didn't let him die. He chose to. Why would you even think you were responsible?"

"Because if I had stayed with him, he wouldn't have had the opportunity to do it."

"Could you have gone with him on that chopper? Could you have stayed by his side every step of the way during his surgery or surgeries? Which, by what you said, I would assume he needed more than one. We only got notified that he died from injuries sustained in a firefight. Then his body was shipped home, and we buried him and mourned his loss. You couldn't have stayed with him during recovery, therapy, or been with him when he finally got home to help him here. Could you?"

"No, but—"

"James made his choice in a moment of weakness. He went back on his promise. That is on him, Lance, not you. I don't blame you; I blame him. He gave up on life, not you." I let go of his face and laid my head on his chest. We sat quietly for a few minutes, and I silently cried as I listened to his heartbeat while I cursed my brother for not having enough courage or faith in his family to deal with his injuries and help him through any troubled times he would have faced with them. Then, I put my focus back on the man in front of me and let the tears flow for James, for my family, and for Lance. The guilt he'd kept to himself all this time. Without lifting my head off his chest, I asked, "Is that part of why you didn't come around when you came home from over there?"

When he didn't answer right away, I wanted to raise my head to look at him, but a part of me was afraid for fear that he had moved on without me instead of regretting what happened with James. He moved, and I felt his lips kiss the top of my head, then he moved away again.

"Yes, because I couldn't face you and your family. I could barely look at myself in the mirror to shave. I knew the signs of self-destruction, but I couldn't stop it. I didn't want to see hate or disgust in your eyes."

"God, Lance, I wouldn't have hated you. James didn't die alone; he had a friend with him. A friend who was fighting for him when he wouldn't even do it for himself."

He wrapped his arms around me and squeezed. "I have issues with the things I've seen and done. I take my meds, and they help, but sometimes, well... even the pills don't keep the stuff away. I hope you can accept me the way I am because, Bailey, I've never stopped loving you."

My head snapped up. He was looking down at me, and his expression was one of hope. "What?"

"I love you. I lost my way for a while, and it has taken me some time to get back to you. You loved me once, and I will do anything to earn it back if you let me. I know I hurt you. You were mine to love, to protect, and I let you down. I wish I could promise that I won't ever hurt you again, but know if it happens, it is unintentional. Going forward, I will fight for you. You were the best part of me then—you are the best part of me now—I want you to be the best part of my future. I know after everything, I have no right to ask, but I am. Fight for me, Bailey. Fight with me—for us."

To say I was speechless at that moment would have been an understatement. But it was more than that. Could I really put the past away as just that, the past, and move forward? His dark brown eyes stared back at me, and when I looked into them, I saw my past and my future. I didn't think there had ever really been a choice since the day I met him. I think the obstacles life placed in our way were to test our bond. Right then, as I stared into his eyes, he'd always been the one. I'd measured every man I dated to him. It was probably why none of my relationships lasted. It was time to see how strong the bond was.

"The past can't be changed, and I'm not sure if I'm strong enough to keep that door closed."

"Bullshit. You are one of the strongest people I know, Bay. Even in your weakest moment, I saw the strength behind the hurt and pain you wore, and even then, I couldn't bring myself to help you through it. I didn't have the capacity to deal with my crap. Fuck, staying away from you didn't help. Nothing I did or tried to do would keep you from surfacing. I'm tired, Bay. I want you. I've always wanted you. My plan was to come at you full steam and give you no choice, but after everything—"

"Shut up, Lance," I cut him off.

"You did not just tell me to shut up." Lance's eyebrows creased and his eyes squinted at me. That was the Lance I remembered.

"Well, you didn't let me finish." I pulled my fingers away from his mouth.

"Go ahead. This is your one chance to put a stop to my pursuit. We agree on one thing: the past needs to stay there. If you're unable to move forward with me, then say it now."

"You've no right to be all pissy because I didn't drop to my knees at your proclamation of love. And for the record, I knew you stood under that tree. I sat on that swing and hoped that you would step out and come to me. I needed my friend then. But you didn't. You stayed away from me. You chose to protect me for whatever misguided reason. I had no choice then because you made it for both of us. You say you're tired. Well, guess what? So am I.

"I survived it all. And what a shocker that I did it without you. I moved forward one step at a time, but I did it on my own. I didn't need you to protect me. I didn't need you to live. What I needed then was for you to love me as much as I loved you. Everything else that came after that would have been a bonus.

"Now, what you didn't let me finish before was I don't think I want to close the door on the past. Yeah, there's hurt there, even a feeling of betrayal, but to lock those away, I would have to lock away the good memories too. And I don't want to forget the first time we held hands, or how I felt the first time we kissed. The nervousness I felt the first time we had sex. To keep those, it is worth the hurt and pain of the other stuff."

"Aww, Bay." I hadn't felt the tears escape my eyes until Lance's hands grabbed my face and his thumbs wiped them away.

"Those experiences were with a young boy. I think I would like to share them again with the man. I never stopped loving you, Lance."

"Damn, Bay," were the only words he said before his lips crashed down on mine. When he pushed his tongue into my mouth, the taste of him filled my senses, and he devoured me until I only held thoughts of him.

Chapter Nine

Devil

What it felt like when my lips touched Bailey's, was indescribable. She was sweet, forgiving, loving, and I may never deserve the woman who straddled my lap, but I was going to take what she was offering.

I hadn't expected Bailey to return my words so easily. Others would probably see everything between us as moving too fast. To me—it was way overdue, and I was bastard enough not to care. A weight lifted off my shoulders and a peace I hadn't felt in a long time settled through me. I would take it, and I would take her.

My tongue took possession of her mouth, touching every crevice, familiarizing itself again with her. I'd taken her virginity, which gave me the title of her first, and I had no misconception that she hadn't been with anyone since. But I damn well would be her last, and she would be mine, making everything in between inconsequential. Bailey moaned into my mouth as I shifted us away enough from the tree to where we laid back on the blanket. My hands ran down her sides, and I cupped her ass and shifted her until she stretched the length of my body, then I rolled us.

Our lips broke apart, and I started my journey down her body to once again familiarize myself with the woman laid beneath me. I kissed from her mouth to her neck and took my time. Eager to learn the differences, but patient enough to take my time. I used my tongue and mouth until I reached her ear, then my teeth bit the lobe and licked the sting away. My cock was hard and ached as it felt the heat from her center pressed against it. With a slight rotation of my hips, I pressed down and the friction as I rubbed my jean-covered cock on her pussy had her pushing up, withering in search of what she needed.

I kissed, nibbled, and licked down her neck and chest until I hit the barrier of her top, stopping my descent. I lifted to my knees, and she grabbed for me.

"Lance, don't stop," she said breathlessly as she clasped my t-shirt in her hands.

"Too many clothes. I want to see all of you. Taste all of you." I removed her hands from my t-shirt and began to remove hers. Sliding it up and over her head as she helped. I unclasped the bra and her large breasts easily exposed themselves to me.

I leaned down on one hand and took my other to touch and squeeze one globe and then the other, and her nipples immediately hardened from the cool air, begging for attention.

"Please, Lance." As soon as Bailey's plea left her lips, I closed my mouth over one breast and used the tip of my tongue to tease the nipple. When I backed away, it was to work my way down her body. My tongue and lips traveled down, only stopping to circle her belly button, then I continued till I hit the waistband of her jeans. Sitting back on my knees again, I unfastened and unzipped the jeans, working them and her underwear off together. The process only stopped long enough to remove her shoes. With her finally naked, I ran my eyes over her, noting the differences between the young girl and the woman before me. I took my hands and ran them down, from her shoulders to her hips, touching curves and dips that weren't there before.

"You're so goddamn beautiful, Bailey," I said as I pushed her thighs apart. She was wet, her pussy lips glistened, showing her arousal in the dimming light.

"Lance, I need. Please," Bailey whispered as she wiggled her hips and tried to close her thighs.

"What do you need, Bay? Tell me. Say it."

"I need you, dammit."

"Not good enough." She huffed and hit the ground beside her.

"Your cock. I need your cock inside me."

"You sure? Sure you don't want my mouth on your pussy?" I asked as I stood and removed my clothes, adding

111

mine to the pile off to the side. I went back to my knees, settling myself between her legs. It would have been easy to give her what she asked for, but the scent of her arousal and the need to taste her overrode her choice. I grabbed her legs, lifted them over my shoulders and then lowered until I laid flat, my mouth inches away from her core.

Resting on my elbows, I slid my hands under Bailey and pulled her toward me as I lowered, closing the distance until my mouth touched her. The first swipe of my tongue had her back arching, the second brought her hands to my hair. The pain from her pulling my hair was just enough to kick my arousal up a notch. I fed off her moans and latched my lips around her clit and sucked. I rolled the hardened nub between my teeth, then used my tongue to lave away the sting.

The taste of her had me wanting more, asking more from her. I slid my hand down until the thumb rested at her back hole. I massaged the area while I pushed my tongue through her slit, reaching her opening to pierce her with my tongue.

The louder she moaned, the faster I thrust my tongue. She was close. So close I felt the quivering of her pussy against my tongue. She released my hair, and I raised my eyes and enjoyed the sight of her with her head thrown back, her hands now on her breasts, squeezing, pinching, and pulling her nipples.

My cock pulsed beneath me. I wanted to sink into Bailey's warmth for my release. I pulled my tongue out and latched my lips around her clit and bit down at the same time I pushed my thumb and breached her back hole.

"Oh, God, Lance!" The dual sensations had Bailey crying out as the orgasm racked her body.

I used my tongue to lap every drop of her juices as she came down from her climax. When her body settled, I released her, slid my hands out from under her and moved until they held my body above her, the weight of my cock resting against her.

When she opened her eyes and they met mine, I slammed my mouth down on hers and pushed my tongue past her lips, giving her a taste of herself. I broke the kiss, my patience exhausted.

"Got to grab a condom." I reached for my jeans, and she grabbed my arm.

"I'm on the pill, and I haven't been with anyone in months. If you can promise me you're clean..."

The woman was full of surprises. The trust she was giving me wasn't missed either.

"I've never been without a condom. Ever. But are you sure?"

"Fuck me, Lance," along with her legs wrapped around me, the heels of her feet pressed against my ass were all I needed. I lined my cock at her entrance, then took her hands with mine and shoved them above her head, then held her wrist with one hand while the other moved beside her to hold my full weight off her. In one hard snap of my hips, I pushed my cock into her pussy, filling her. Then I gave her time to adjust to my size. She was tight, wet, and warm, the walls squeezing my dick just to the edge between pleasure and pain.

She dug her heels into my ass cheeks as she shifted beneath, the movement allowing me to sink further in until the tip of my cock touched her cervix. The pressure surrounding my cock eased, and I knew her body was ready. She was made for me and would take everything I gave to her.

I pulled out and thrusted back into her until Bailey's head bent back as far as it would go and her back arched. I knew then I wouldn't last long.

"Not going to last long, baby. Hope you're ready," it was all I got out. I released her wrist, used my hands and pulled her legs from around me, pushed them until her legs were bent at the knees and her feet sat flat on the blanket. The position opened her wider to me. I used the advantage of holding her legs in the position to give me the resistance I needed to hold me up while I pounded into her. In, out, her cries growing louder as I took. Even then, I wanted more.

"Give me everything, Bay. I want it all. Fuck me back. Show me this is the only pussy I'll ever need."

"Damn you, Lance!" Bailey yelled before she pushed her hips up to meet me. The sound of skin hitting skin resonated the air. For every groan, for every moan, the gap between our past and the present grew smaller. The woman was and would be everything to me. I shoved deep one last time. My balls drew up, and my orgasm racked my body as my seed filled Bailey, marking her. Her own orgasm followed, causing her to spasm around my cock, squeeze every drop from me.

After I pulled out, I rolled to the side and pulled her in my arms while we tried to catch our breath.

When Bailey shivered, I knew it was time to get her inside.

"You're cold. Let's get dressed."

"Okay, if I can move," she said, then chuckled, never opening her eyes.

I stood and moved to grab our clothes, and she rolled, grabbed the blanket and folded it over her body.

"Come on. Not sure you want to wear that blanket back to my house, though." I chuckled as I dressed. I put my boots on as she stood and reached for her clothes.

"I should go home. Will you walk me to my car?"

"Oh, I will walk you to your car, but not right now. We are going to my house. I'm going to fix you something warm to drink, and then I'm going to take you to my bedroom and fuck you in my bed. Did you seriously think I was going to have you once and let you go home, Bay?"

"Lance! Stop talking to me like that." Bailey might have meant it, but I was more apt to believe that none of her other men had talked to her like that because the sucking in of her bottom lip and the teeth biting down on said lip told a different story.

"If I thought my talk bothered you, I might consider using nicer words, but I would bet money you're wet again with just the thought of what I might do to you when I get you to my house. I got one thing in mind, however, if I'm right, it is going to take a little working up to."

"Stop it!" I moved toward her, and she backed up.

"Why are you moving away? I just wanted to check to see if you were wet." She backed away until I had her between the tree and me. "Are you? Is your pussy wet, Bay, wanting my cock again or my tongue?"

"Lance," came out on a pant. I grabbed the blanket, reached for her hand, and we started toward my house.

When we entered, the door hadn't fully closed, and I was leading her to the stairs.

"I thought you were going to get me something warm to drink?" Bailey said over her shoulder and smiled at me as we walked up the stairs.

"Yeah, that is going to have to wait until I have you one more time." I grabbed her ass with my hands, and she squealed.

"You give this to anyone?" She knew what I was asking because I squeezed her ass for emphasis. The whispered no didn't surprise me. "Going to give it to me, though, right? I want all of you, Bay. Including that."

She didn't say anything in reply as I walked to my room.

"Don't shut down on me. I will not take what you don't want to give me, and I'm not asking you to give it to me now. Got to work up to it, get you ready for it. Okay? You don't like what I'm doing when the time comes, we stop."

"Alright."

"Good. Now get those clothes back off so I can show you again what you mean to me."

We stripped down, and I took her to my bed and showed her just that. After she curled into me and sleep took us, I don't know how long we laid there before my cell rang and woke us up.

"Yeah? Are you fucking shitting me? Okay. Meet you out front." I hung up with Crusher and leaned over and kissed Bailey before getting out of bed.

"If you have to go, I'm going to head out too." Bailey got out of bed and started dressing.

"Stay here and wait for me. It shouldn't take too long. Something is going on at the club, and we have to go check it out."

"That's fine. I really should go home and check on my mom."

"Okay. We can follow you home before we go to the club." I sat on the bed and put my boots on. "Bakery closed tomorrow, right?"

"Yes, Mom closes two Sundays a month. Which is good. I've got a few things I need to get done."

"I want to see you again tomorrow. I've got Church in the afternoon. Can you get your stuff done before four?"

"Probably."

"Good, I'll text and let you know what time. Pack a bag. I want you to stay the night with me."

"Lance, I don't know if I—"

"Come on, Bay. Monday I leave on club business, and I'm going to be gone for a few days. I want to spend some time with you before I go. I'm leaving early so you can get up and have plenty of time to make it to the bakery." Bailey stood after she put her shoes on and walked into the bathroom without answering me. I put on my vest and grabbed up my keys and shoved my phone in my pocket while I waited for her to come out. When she did, I noticed her face was washed, and her hair fixed back into a ponytail.

"Okay," was all she said when she walked out. I moved to stand in front of her, and she looked up at me.

"Thank you. I've missed you more than you will ever know, and I don't want to waste any more time." Bailey smiled, and I leaned down and took her lips.

"Dev, we need to go!" I leaned my forehead against hers and groaned.

"I knew I should have locked that door." Bailey chuckled, and I stepped away. "Let's go before Coast comes up here."

"I have a key, dumbass!"

Bailey walked out of the room, and I followed. When we stepped outside, the others were ready and waited on their bikes while I mounted mine and Bailey got on behind me. We stopped long enough for her to get in her car, and then the six of us followed her until she was parked and safely inside her house.

The next stop was Soft Tails.

Chapter Ten

Devil

We pulled into the parking lot at Soft Tails, and bikes were lined up. Most of the club had to be inside.

"Goddamn, what the hell is going on?" Crusher said after we parked and started toward the entrance of Soft Tails. The closer we got, the louder the sounds. By the time we reach the door, music could be heard, along with the whoops and yells of the men inside.

"I swear I'm going to kick the asses of anyone who has trashed shit inside. They're going to be fined and pay for any damages," Crusher said and grabbed hold of the handle on the door.

"They pulled my ass out of a warm bed and away from my ol' lady. I might kick an ass or two on principal."

"Brax didn't tell you what was going on when he called?" Jag asked as Crusher pulled the door open.

"Nah, just said we'd want to get down here because the place was out of control. Then I had to fight with Carly because her ass wanted to come in case we needed backup." Crusher shook his head, and we entered the club.

Brax stood just inside the entrance when we walked in, and I looked around and didn't see any destruction. Other than the music being loud, everyone in the place seemed to be enjoying themselves as they drank and watched the girls on the stage.

"What the fuck? Why were we called?" Crusher yelled out over the music.

"I got told to call you and tell you to get down here. They didn't tell me why, Prez," Brax answered.

We stood there for a few minutes and watched. Stroker, Preacher, Cruz, and Flyboy sat a table with Wild Bill and Keg.

"We got woke up for this shit!" Speed yelled.

"And where in the fucking hell is my dad?" Flirt asked.

"I don't know," Jag said, then looked around. "Isn't that Romeo at the bar?" Jag pointed to where Romeo stood leaning on the bar as he talked with Stem, who was bartending. Flirt started toward his dad.

"Hell, maybe Romeo knows what the hell is going on," I said.

"Go with Flirt. We can go check with the others," Crusher started toward the table where his dad and the others sat.

"Hell," I mumbled and followed Flirt toward the bar. I noticed as we weaved between the tables, the members we passed by stopped talking. Something was up. When we reached Romeo, he looked up at us and saluted with the beer bottle he held in his hand.

"What brings you boys out at this time of night?" Romeo asked, looked at his watch, then continued. "Or morning, I guess." Flirt moved in front of his dad.

"Why did we get woken up to come down here? Nothing is fucking going on." Flirt fanned his arm out to include the whole place. Romeo's lips twitched as he looked at Flirt.

"Well, I would love to share, but I haven't been here long myself." Romeo took a drink of his beer.

"Anything happen before we got here?" I asked Stem.

"Nope. Typical night," Stem answered and then moved down the bar to wait on Boss and Turk as they walked up.

"You left with them, so where have you been?" Flirt asked, and Romeo looked at him and then at me.

"I took Claire home. Stayed and talked with her until about twenty minutes ago."

"You were with Bailey's mom? I thought you were dropping her off?" I asked and frowned.

"I've known Claire a long time. We went to school together. What is the big deal?" Romeo asked me.

"Claire is bouncing back—" Romeo interrupted, cutting me off.

"You think I don't know that? I'm glad you came to your senses where Bailey is concerned, but—"

"Dad," Flirt said and stopped his dad from continuing. Romeo looked over at Flirt.

"No, you boys get the respect for being this club's leadership, but you don't get to stick your nose where it doesn't belong." Romeo faced me again and continued where he left off. "I know everything Claire and her daughter have been through because I was here. I stood on the outside and watched them at their lowest, and then I witnessed the strength in both of them as they pulled themselves up. Not saying any of this to hurt you, Devil, or any of you. But each one of you acts like you are the only ones who has seen or done nasty shit. The only ones to make bad choices. Grow up, pull up your big boy underwear and look around you. Most of the men in this club have served in the military at one time or another. They've lost wives, ol' ladies, friends, comrades." Romeo didn't give us a chance to answer. "I'm going to go sit with my brothers," was said before he turned to walk off.

"What crawled up your ass, old man?" Flirt asked, and Romeo kept walking but turned his head and spoke over his shoulder.

"Nothing other than you don't have the market on regrets." Romeo kept walking, and Flirt looked over at me.

"What the hell was that supposed to mean?" I asked, and Flirt shrugged.

"Who knows? I need a beer. These old men give me a headache." Flirt hit the bar to get Stem's attention.

"You think that is how they felt when we did shit growing up?" I chuckled. Stem sat Flirt and me a beer on the bar.

"Yeah, and a lot worse." I nodded in agreement, and we turned to head to where the others were. As we approached, the music shut off. Stroker stood and shook Speed's hand and patted his back, then Wild Bill stood and did the same. When I looked at Crusher, he wore a smile.

"You couldn't have Brax tell me that when he called?" Crusher asked as Flirt and I reached the table. I went and stood behind my dad's chair.

"Hell no because you wouldn't have come. The only way to pull you away from your ol' ladies." Stroker laughed.

"We could've done this later," Speed said.

"What is going on?" Flirt asked.

"They wanted to celebrate Sami accepting Speed's proposal," Jag answered.

"And we couldn't do that later?" I asked, and my dad started chuckling.

"Did we interrupt your time with Bailey?" he said over his shoulder to me

"Yeah, you did," I answered.

"Get over it. Hopefully, Speed only proposes to one woman." My dad laughed when Speed glared at him.

"They wanted to do it while Keg and I were here. We are heading back to Haven tomorrow afternoon," Wild Bill,

Sami's dad and president of Haven, said. While the men explained, the other members around us laughed.

"Hey, maybe you boys can implement this into the by-laws. We could call it the ball and chain get-together." Stroker chuckled at his own joke.

"I'll get right on that. Now I thought you said we were here to celebrate. Start the music up!" Crusher yelled.

"First round is on me. I couldn't have handpicked a better man for my little girl." Wild Bill held up the bottle of beer he already had in the air, and everyone whooped and whistled. The music started back up, the girls started dancing, and beers started being handed out.

The last thing I remembered was telling my dad the next party would be mine.

Chapter Eleven

Devil

Fuck! I opened my eyes a crack, then shut them quickly when the light that shined through my window hit my eyeballs. I swallowed, and my mouth felt like someone had shoved it full of cotton. I groaned and rolled over onto my stomach and buried my head under the pillow.

"Damn, you need to open a fucking window. You need to get up and take a hot shower and sweat the rest of that shit out of you. The price you pay for shooting Jose and chasing it with beer. That was asking for a disaster," Coast said, then I heard the window open.

"Can you not talk so fucking loud? How did I get home? And why are you not in the same shape?"

"Someone had to stay sober. Then we had a problem because everyone had their bikes. So yeah, we probably want to stay away from the women for a while. Sami and Carly were called with some of the other ol' ladies. It wasn't pretty. It shocked me when Bailey showed up, but Carly said that she should see what she's getting into and share their pain."

"Wait! What? Bailey came to Soft Tails?"

"Get the pillow off your head. I just said that she was there. She brought you home. Sad that most are going to have to have their ol' ladies drop them off at Church so they can pick up their bikes. Three-fourths of the club's bikes are still parked at Soft Tails."

"Was she mad?" I rolled back over, and without opening my eyes, I sat up on the side of the bed and leaned my arms on my knees and hung my head. Nothing like getting your woman back and on the same day she gets to drag your drunk ass home. I took a deep breath. "Goddammit, did I spill a bottle of Jose on me? Fuck."

"Nope, that would be all you. You and Roscoe bet each other on who could shoot the most Jose and keep standing. It was sad, brother. And Bailey wasn't mad from what I could tell." Coast flopped down in the chair in the corner.

"Good. Is Roscoe okay? Did he fall or something?" Coast started laughing, and I raised my head, and the movement made me groan.

"Really? Sue came and picked him up if it makes you feel better. He could not ride his bike, but fall? Roscoe's old ass walked out on his own. You, brother, it was embarrassing. You fell off the stool. Your dad had to pick you up, and Bailey helped get you out to her car."

"I need a shower, and to brush my teeth." I stood and made my way to the bathroom, and that was when I noticed I was still in all my clothes. The only thing removed was my boots.

"Good. We got to be at Church in an hour. The others said they would meet us there. Wild Bill and Keg were pulling out to head back to Haven when I walked over here."

"Shit, Church should be fun." Coast laughed, and I flipped him off over my shoulder as I hit the door with my heel and it closed behind me. First, I needed water and a couple aspirin, then a nice hot shower.

I finished my shower and was dressed in fifteen minutes to spare when Coast and I walked out the front door of my house, and Bailey's car pulled up.

"Thought you might need a ride into town since you don't have your bike." Bailey's lips twitched. "I added you to my chore list for the day."

"Bailey, I'm so sorry they called, and you had to come out last night." When her face fell, I wondered what I'd said wrong.

"Oh, well. I just thought it would help you out. You mumbled about your bike while I was taking off your boots. I didn't even think that there would be plenty of people to run you to the club." Before I could reply to Bailey, Coast cleared his throat.

"Going to go grab my bike since Bailey's here. Be back, and I'll follow you two." Coast headed toward his house, and I waited until he was a distance away.

"Out of the car."

"What?"

"Out of the car." I pulled the door open the second time I said it and waited for her to step out. She huffed, exited the car, and tried to move around me. I boxed her in with my arms on each side of her while my hands rested on the car. "You can come to my house anytime. Nothing would make me happier. Do you understand?"

"Yes."

"Good. Now," I bent my head and took her mouth. I held back from devouring her. It would have been so easy. Instead, I backed away as Coast rode up, "that we have that settled. I'll be looking forward to make-up sex after I pick you up this afternoon."

"Yeah, go ahead and think that." Bailey skirted around the car and got in on the passenger side, and I folded myself into the driver's side. Fucking cages.

On the drive into town, I talked to Bailey, and she answered in short, clipped responses.

"You trying to piss me off? Think that is going to stop me from fucking you when I get you back to my house this afternoon?"

"I don't think I want to come to your house today. You're a jerk." Bailey stared out the side window and refused to look in my direction.

I laughed and pulled into the lot at Soft Tails. I pulled the car up to the front and got out and waited for her to come around the car. Bailey didn't speak or look at me, she just got in and reached to pull the door close, but I still held onto it.

"Don't you have a meeting to go to?" She looked up at me, and I smirked.

"Yes, and when I get done with it, I will be at your mom's house. If you don't have a bag packed, that is up to you. But you will be following me home." Bailey's mouth opened, and I didn't give her a chance to say a word. "Don't be ready, and I'll show you what a big jerk I am when I toss you over my shoulder and haul your ass out of the house. See you in a little while, baby." I closed the car door and walked into the club without looking back.

"Damn, I don't know what you said to Bailey, but I was waiting for your ass to go up in flames." Coast hit me on the back when he came in the club behind me.

"Ah, just a little foreplay." I chuckled.

"Another brother down. You are a goner for that woman," Coast said as we headed to the front where the others stood, speaking to some members along the way.

"Yeah, I am. Shit, I think I was two minutes after I walked into the bakery last week. Know what, Coast?" I lowered my voice.

"What?"

"I could not care less. She's it for me."

"Glad to hear it. Happy for you, brother." We reached the others, and Coast stepped off to the side.

"You're alive," my dad said as I sat in the chair beside Jag, who laughed.

"Wasn't too sure about that when I woke up."

"I feel your pain. Ally ran into the room this morning and jumped on me. And I had firsthand experience of what Sami is going through with morning sickness. As I hugged that bowl, I considering drowning myself." Everyone in hearing distance laughed at Speed.

"You boys are lightweights. I got up this morning to eggs, bacon, and biscuits and gravy," Roscoe said, and Crusher, Speed, Flirt, and I groaned.

"Alright, let's get Church underway. My bed is still calling to me." The room got quiet when Crusher spoke. He started with Jas going back home to the Ops.

Then Flirt covered the money and where the club was sitting as far as finances and what was predicted for the next month. The four-bike contract we just signed two weeks ago for Black Hawk Custom Bikes would put a good chunk into the coffer. After current business was over, that was when any new business went on record.

"Turk and Boss, you had something you wanted to run past the club?" Crusher asked. Turk stood so everyone in the room could hear.

"Boss and I have been looking into opening a cannabis shop. The return on the initial startup cost is laid out in the proposal you have. The cost of purchasing the product is down, considering we grow it. Of course, a lot of the plants we have are allocated to the government, but we bought the land that runs the length of our land at the back. That land could be used to grow the crop for the shop."

"We'll look over the plan. Run some numbers and then at the next meeting we will do a vote on how much will be kicked in on the startup cost. We have one more thing to take care of today. Brax, can you come up here?"

Brax walked from the back of the room, and as he approached the table, the rest of us stood.

"You've been prospecting with Black Hawk for almost a year. You've done everything you've been asked to do, no questions. You pitch in wherever you are needed, so as of today, you'll be a full member. Also, you can thank Flirt for ratting you out. Every prospect has a sponsor. Flirt was yours. So, I'm going to let him do the honors. Thanks for your loyalty toward Black Hawk, its members, and its leadership."

Flirt walked around the table and stood in front of Brax and held up a vest with the Black Hawk patch. Brax took off the vest he wore, showing he was a prospect, and put on his new one. When he faced the rest of the members, most got to see his club name written on the front. Cheers and whooping came from the others, and Brax smiled.

"Damn, I don't know what to say. Thank you, it is an honor to be a member of the Black Hawk MC doesn't seem enough just to say that after everything you've done for me," Brax said, then looked at Stroker, Flyboy, Preacher, Cruz, and Romeo. "To the former leadership, I want you to know I appreciate you taking in a broken man, giving him a home, and making him feel a part of something again." Brax turned and faced us. "And to the new leadership, I pledge my loyalty and support. Your friendship since I rode through the gates with Flirt came easily, and it has meant a lot."

When Ghost finished, Crusher brought Church to an end. We toasted our new member, which several did with soda, to include me, then everyone started to leave. After the last member was gone, that was when I and the others headed out.

The anticipation of having Bailey in my arms again and all to myself had me on my bike and headed toward her house in minutes.

Chapter Twelve

Bailey

"Better have a bag ready. Haul my ass out. Whatever."

"Bailey, what are you in there mumbling about?" My mom stepped into my room.

"Lance, he can be such an ass. I don't remember that about him. I must have blocked that part of his personality out." My mom moved to stand beside me, and when I glanced over at her, she was smiling. "What?"

"I can open the bakery in the morning if you don't want to make the trek from Black Hawk that early," she said, then picked up the shirt that laid on my bed and folded it. The smile was still on her face.

"Do you find this amusing?" I glared at her.

"Aww, sweetie. How can I not? You are mumbling and griping, yet... packing a bag to stay at his house." My mom started laughing, and I couldn't hold back, I started laughing too as I shoved the shirt she'd folded in the bag and zipped it.

"He drives me crazy! One minute he is this loving man, then the next, he is arrogant and bossy. Oh, and he thinks everything can be solved with sex!" I went on a rant, and my mom started laughing harder and sat down on the bed. That's when I realized what I had voiced, and I felt my face heat.

"Bailey, do you know how hard that probably was to tell you about James? He felt responsible, even though James was the one who chose his own fate. But I believe it was more he felt he let *you* down. That is why he couldn't face you, honey." I leaned over and hugged my mom.

"I wish I hadn't told you about James. You've been through so much."

"No, I'm glad you did. Does my heart hurt because your brother didn't have enough faith in his family? Yes. But in the end, Bailey, we all answer for ourselves."

"Yeah, that is pretty much what I told Lance." I heard a motorcycle outside, and then it went silent.

"I think your young man is here for you," my mom said and stood. "And to answer your earlier rant. Usually, when a man can bring every emotion pouring from you, means he gets to you. He is comfortable enough to show you every side of him. Know the emotion I've not seen from or have never seen from you when you talk about Lance?"

"No." I frowned at my mom, but she smiled back at me.

"Fear. No matter how he acts, responds to things—you are not scared that he would ever physically hurt you."

"True, but verbally is different." Mom stopped at the entrance to my bedroom just as the doorbell chimed.

"He is a man. They say dumb shit sometimes. But then that is when you let them make it up to you. I'll get the door while you grab your things."

"Some things can't be taken back, by a grand gesture!" I yelled as my mom walked out.

"No, a woman never forgets, but that doesn't mean you can't enjoy them using sex and thinking they're getting their way!"

"Mom!"

"Older, Bailey. Not dead!"

I stood in the middle of my bedroom and stared at the empty doorway. My mother never ceased to amaze me. I heard her greet Lance and invite him in. I grabbed my purse and bag and headed toward the door. When I reached the living room where he stood talking with my mom, he turned, and his eyes ran over me. As they touched on the bag in my hand, I watched the smile form. His eyes traveled back up to mine, and the desire that reflected at me was staggering. My stomach tightened with the promise his eyes held. Suddenly, I couldn't get out of there fast enough and hoped the drive to his house went quickly.

It was like the bastard knew what I thought as I watched his smile turn to a smirk. He turned back toward my mom, and in less than two minutes, he said bye, told her to call if any problems popped up, then had me in my car as I waited for him to get on his bike. He waved for me to pull out so he could follow.

With thoughts of him and what he might do to me at his house, I pulled out.

We barely made it in the house. My bag hit the floor along with my purse being snatched out of my hand and throw in the same direction. The door closed when he pushed me back against it and started kissing me. Lance only broke the kiss long enough to pull my shirt over my head and unclasp my bra to join it, then his lips were back on mine. My pants were more of a problem, but they didn't keep him from his mission. He broke the kiss and stepped back and pushed them all the way down. My panties went with them. Shoes were removed, and I stood naked while he was fully clothed.

Lance stood back up and, with his lips close to mine and his eyes focused on me, a shiver ran through me.

"I don't know if I can go slow. I want you too damn much."

I ran my fingers through his hair and closed the distance between us until our lips met. His lips and tongue dominated mine, leaving me breathless. Neither of us could get enough. He ran a hand down my side until he reached my hip. Goosebumps formed on my skin where his hands touched me.

Lance grabbed the cheeks of my butt and squeezed and caressed. When he lifted me up, I wrapped my legs around his waist, my bare pussy making contact with the material of his jeans. My clit throbbed, and I shifted to gain a better grip with my legs and make contact with his very hardened cock. I rolled my hips, and he groaned. The desire in his eyes had darkened the brown to almost black. His nostrils flared and his arms adjusted until only one held me while the other hand moved between us to unzip his pants.

Lance's cock popped free and laid between my legs, hard, and the heat of its touch had me shifting. Lance pushed his hips forward, and his cock slid through my folds. He groaned when I tightened on his length.

"Fuck!" Lance yelled and leaned his forehead on my shoulder.

"Please," I whispered, then gasped when he thrust into me.

"Oh God, that feels good. You are so warm and wet for me."

I leaned my head back against the door. "Stop talking and fuck me, Lance." I pushed down on him.

"Damn, I like when you talk dirty. And I really like that my girl's pussy is greedy and can't get enough."

Lance moved back, and his cock slid out, only leaving the head inside. With the snap of his hips, he pushed into the hilt again and my back arched, my shoulders hitting the door. He pulled out and thrust in again. His size stretched me almost to the point of pain.

I pulled his hair and rolled my hips and flexed, tightening my pussy around him. His hands gripped me so hard that I was sure there would be fingerprint bruises on my butt cheeks.

"Tight as a glove, but this pussy was made for me."

I moaned as Lance picked up speed and, with each thrust, he pulled me down to meet him. He pounded into me, and the only things heard were our skin touching and our heavy breathing.

"I'm so close!" I yelled, my orgasm just out of reach.

"Me too." Lance breathed out, shifted until he was able to get a hand between us. I let go of his hair to hold on to his shoulders.

Lance rubbed my swollen clit and matched the speed to his thrust, moving me closer to explosion. When he pinched my clit and bit down on my shoulder and shoved to the hilt, my body shook from the climax. My pussy spasmed around him as he reached his own orgasm and filled me.

Then stayed connected as we tried to catch our breaths. "You can put me down."

"Plan on it. Just not here." He kept us connected as he turned away from the door and walked to the stairs. "You got to hold my pants up, or this could turn ugly fast."

When we reached his bedroom was when he pulled out and let me slide down his body till my feet hit the floor. Only then did he step back and start removing his clothes.

No words came as I watched him strip each piece of his clothing away. His skin was tan and smooth, and I wanted nothing more than to lick my way down from his lips and then follow the dark trail of hair that led to his cock. I licked my lips, and his cock twitched.

"You can suck my cock later, Bay. Right now, I need back inside you."

"You're insatiable." My eyes were glued to his cock as it hardened in front of me. Lance's hand came down and wrapped around it and stroked up and down on it until I watched a bead of pre-cum form on the tip.

"Get on the bed. Hands and knees, and your ass in the air." I snapped my eyes up to his on the demand.

"Kind of bossy." The black took over his eyes again.

"Yeah. You'll get used to it. Because you know whatever I do to you will feel good. Whether it's my mouth eating you out or my dick stuffing you fully."

I rubbed my thighs together when my pussy spasmed at his words. Lance didn't miss the movement.

"That's right, even your body knows. Get on the bed, Bay. Don't make me tell you again. I'm barely hanging on right now." I turned and climbed on the bed and got in the position he told me to and waited.

"Scoot to the bottom." I did as he asked. The bed dipped on one side, and when I looked down under my arm, I saw one of his knees resting on the bed. Then everything left my mind, and I grabbed at the bedding as a finger was pushed inside me. Another was added, and after a few ins and outs, they slid out and up, taking my juices with them.

I jerked a little when Lance moved his knee off the bed, stood behind me, and touched my back hole and circled it. I didn't know if I was ready for that yet.

"Hold on, not going to put my cock there yet." I squeezed the bedding in my hands as his finger circled the rim. I felt pressure, but no pain when he breached the surrounding muscle with the tip. "Relax, baby."

I felt his cock at the entrance to my pussy, and he slowly pushed in. When he started to move, it was slow at first, then Lance increased the speed of his thrust. The finger in the back hole he moved in and out too. Only pushing inside the barrier to the first knuckle.

"Oh yeah, that's it, relax. You might think this is dirty or forbidden, but your body is telling me different. I can feel your juices surrounding my cock. I can feel your asshole tightening around my finger, trying to take it deeper."

"Stop talking like that." The words came out breathless, proving me wrong in what I said. The different sensations felt good. I wanted Lance to take me, all of me.

"Don't lie, Bay. Your body is letting me know what you want to deny. You like me talking nasty. You like me pushing your limits. We'll get there. Maybe not today, but one day you will be begging me to take your ass and make it mine." Lance pushed his finger deeper as he thrusted in and out of me.

"I can't hold off much longer. Take us both, baby. Use your fingers to rub your clit." I moved one hand under me until I reached my clit. It was hard and sensitive to the touch. When I pressed two of my fingers down and rubbed back and forth, it was just what I needed. The orgasm was on me and racked my body. Lance didn't go over with me and continued to fuck me through my orgasm.

I pushed back with each of his thrusts. A foot hit the bed, and the new angle had his sack hitting my clit each time he bottomed out. I moved my hand and went back to holding onto the blankets. I was going to be sore the next day, but no way would I regret it.

The pounding he was giving me lasted long enough to have yet another orgasm build and this time when it hit, Lance went with me.

The orgasm began to build, and the walls of my pussy tightened around Lance. He pounded into me, and on his last thrust, he pushed his finger all the way into my ass.

The scream that tore from my throat had nothing to do with pain and everything to do with the man laid over me. His own yell filled the air as his seed filled me and his cock twitched.

As I came down from my bliss, I couldn't believe the man behind me. The things he made me feel were almost indescribable.

Lance pulled out, and as he went toward the bathroom, I moved up on the bed. When he came back, it was with a cloth, and he began to take care of me. The warm cloth doing wonders for sensitive areas. He took the cloth back to the bathroom and joined me on the bed.

"Gotta get a little sleep. Glad you are here, Bay. Love you, baby." Lance yawned and pulled me into his arms.

"Love you, too," I said, but then chuckled when the only response I got was a soft snore. I closed my eyes and enjoyed the feel of being in his arms. It wasn't long until sleep had taken me too.

Chapter Thirteen

Devil

I was going to owe my woman a lot went I got back. We'd fallen asleep after I rutted on her like a damn bull. No dinner, not even breakfast the next morning because we pulled out under darkness after a call about some stranger asking fucking questions about the club at Stu's One-Stop at the edge of town. Crusher notified us all and said we should get an earlier start than we planned.

The call had woken Bailey, and she stretched and rolled on top of me. As I laid there enjoying the feel of her body before I had to get up and leave her, I willed my cock to go down. When she giggled, I looked down at her.

"After last night, I'm surprised he's able to get hard." She moved her hand down and wrapped it around my dick, and I groaned.

"Bay, unless you want me to sink balls deep into you again, you might want to let him go." I reached to remove her hand, but she tightened her gripped and pumped up and down on my cock. My good intention left. She slid her body down, and when she rested between my thighs, she dropped her head, and her tongue came out and circled the head. Christ, my back arched as she licked and sucked the tip into her mouth. I reached down and ran my fingers through her hair. She hummed around the tip, and my head bent back, then she released me only to run her tongue on the underside from base to tip, then she circled the head. A drop of pre-cum rolled down the side, and her tongue moved and scooped it up like she would do on a dripping ice cream cone.

With one hand wrapped around my dick, she took her other hand and played with my balls. Her mouth opened wide, and she took my cock deep. The move had me reaching down with my other hand to hold her head between them.

While I thrust my hips, I held her still, careful not to gag her. I fucked her mouth, and I knew she was as turned on as I was when she moaned. I felt the vibrations all the way down into my balls.

"Goddamn, you keep surprising me. You like me fucking your mouth as much as that pussy, Bay?" I took the moan as a yes. The hand she still had on my balls rolled them around, and she used her finger and touched the underside spot. The action made me shove up and deep into her mouth until the tip touched the back of her throat. When she didn't gag, I pulled out and did it again.

I couldn't take my eyes off my dick as it tunneled in and out of her mouth. When the tingle started, I knew I was close.

"I don't want to come in your mouth, baby. I pulled out and moved my hands from her head to under her arms and lifted her up and over until still laid on her back. My weight was on my knees as I straddled her waist. Bailey's breasts bounced, drawing my attention. The sight of her peaked nipples told me my woman was into it what I was doing. I took my hand and only had to stroke my cock twice before I sprayed my come all over her breasts. I watched a shiver go through her as I pumped until every drop was wrung from my dick. It might make me an asshole, but the sight of her breasts and nipples glistening with my come seemed right. I took my hands and rubbed the come over her chest, squeezing her breasts and tweaking her nipples as I did. When Bailey's eyes closed, I slid down her body until I laid between her legs. I grabbed each leg and pushed them up, bending them at the knee with her feet flat on the bed. With my hands positioned to hold her legs in place, I dropped onto my stomach.

"Hold yourself open, Bay." When her eyes opened, and she looked down at me, I added, "Reach between your legs and hold those pretty pussy lips open for me. I want to see every glistening inch of you. I don't want to miss one drop of your juices."

When she hesitated at first, as if she wasn't going to do what I asked, I leaned down and made a pass with my tongue through her lips.

"Don't you like feeling my tongue run through your lips, or me sucking your clit?" Bailey's hands came down, and she used her fingers to spread herself before me.

I licked her from back to front over and over. I fucked her with my tongue like I would with my dick. Her knees pressed into my ears and her hips thrust up and rolled as she tried to chase my tongue to get it where she wanted and needed it.

After one more swipe, I moved my focus to her clit. My tongue circled it, and I knew that was going to send her over the edge when her hips pushed up, searching for more. My dick was hard as steel from her moaning and thrashing. I moved my hand to her mound and used the thumb to rub circles and keep pressure on her clit. When her head bowed back, I knew she was ready. I moved back up her body until I rested on my forearms. Then I lined my dick up at her entrance to her pussy.

"I can't imagine anything in life feeling better than waking up next to you," I said, then slammed into her.

Bailey's body convulsed and shook, her back arched, her head went back. As her orgasm rolled through, I took more. I pounded into her. Her warm and wet pussy contracting around me.

"I don't think I can take anymore," Bailey said breathlessly, but I didn't stop. I pushed her more.

"Yeah, you can. You will. Not going to see you for a few days. Going to take the taste of and the feel of you with me." I grabbed one of her legs and lifted it up to my hip, and I drove into her until I felt her body betray her words. "That's it, Bailey, one more."

She thrust her hips up, and I went so deep I felt the tip of my cock touch her cervix. I yelled out, and she screamed, and we went over together.

When her body settled down, I pulled out, picked her up, and carried her to the bathroom to get cleaned up.

Then I left her standing on my porch with Shakes and Dare and the others as Ghost drove the truck with Jas inside and Jag and I followed behind on our bikes.

That had been day one. We'd driven through Oregon and stopped before we crossed the border into Cali and spent the first night. After the drive, we'd eaten dinner and went into our rooms and crashed.

The next day was an early start again, but I'd used the memories of Bailey the morning before to pass the time.

At one of our stops, I even texted the guy holding my mom's shit for an address and told him I could stop by on Wednesday and pick it up. The text back said he expected back some money for taking care of her shit. Yeah, that little prick was going to be in for a surprise. I'll see what he had, see what shit my mom had gotten herself into and then me, Jag, and Ghost would make the two-day ride back home.

After another long ass day of riding, we'd finally pulled into San Jose that evening. It was getting dark just as we found the motel the Ops were to meet us at. We parked the truck and bikes and went in to get our rooms. We'd be staying there overnight. So would the Ops.

"Damn, we are getting soft. My ass is numb," Jag said, and Jas giggled as we walked out of the motel office to head to our rooms.

"I feel you. We haven't been on a long ride in months. When we get back, we should talk to the others to see if we can take a few days, maybe ride up to Canada."

"That sounds good. Ghost, would you be up for it?" Jag asked.

"Damn straight I would. I haven't made it to Canada yet. Washington has been the furthest I've been. I grew up in LA until I went into the military." Ghost and the rest of us turned when we heard pipes from a couple of motorcycles in the distance.

Two came into view, with an SUV behind them. When Jas started jumping up and down, we knew it had to be the Ops. The bikes pulled in, and the SUV followed. The two men on the bikes dismounted and when the one got both his feet on the ground, he had just enough time to catch Jas as she jumped into his arms. Jas finished with one and moved to the next man and did the same as two women stepped out of the SUV.

"What the fuck, Jas? We should get the first hugs, not those two assholes," the one woman yelled.

"Umm...yeah, I think it's a good idea to keep their women away from ours," Jag whispered, and Ghost and I laughed.

Jas screeched, "Harmony! Moon!" And the two Ops men laughed and made their way to us.

"I'm Cajun, one of Jas's stepdads. This is Fork, our VP, and his ol' lady, Harmony," Cajun pointed to one woman walking toward us, then pointed to the other woman as they got closer, but he didn't have time to say her name.

"Luna?" Ghost asked, and the woman turned her head away from Jas and looked at him.

"Oh. My. God. Braxton Samuel Carver!" the woman yelled. Jag, the Ops men, and I watched the two and wore the same expression of what the hell? Fork's ol' lady didn't seem to have a problem speaking.

"You know this guy, Moon?" she asked and looked Ghost up and down. "Damn, girl, you'd have to climb him like a tree, but then again, if all his parts are portioned, it would be worth it."

"Harmony, I'm standing right here," Fork said with a sigh.

"Please, I'm carrying your and Creed's devil spawn. What more do you want?"

Ghost watched the woman he called Luna, and Jag and I watched the Ops VP and his ol' lady.

"So, who is the man, Moon?" Harmony asked again.

"I'm Ghost, Luna and I grew up together." As soon as Ghost spoke Harmony moved in front of the woman she called Moon and Ghost had referred to as Luna.

149

"Is this the motherfucker who slept with your girl and broke your heart?" Harmony asked and didn't wait for Luna/Moon to answer. "I should get my knives out of the truck a cut your ass." Then Fork caught Harmony's arm before she could turn around and head back to the truck and he bent and whispered in her ear. Harmony said loud enough for us to hear, "Fine. But if my homegirl needs me. I am there! Now get us some rooms, I'm tired. Us girls will share a room, and you and Cajun can share a room." Fork was ready to reply, but then stopped beside Jag and me before he went into the office to get the rooms.

"You got ol' ladies?" he asked.

"No," Jag answered, and Fork patted his back.

"Don't. Life is easier."

"I heard that!"

"Of course you did. I'll take the couch when I get home."

"Damn straight you will."

Fork looked at me. "She really is nice. The pregnancy is making her crazier than normal." He headed into the office.

Cajun and Jas laughed, and I had a feeling the VP had told a big tale about his ol' lady. While we had been listening to their banter, no one noticed that Ghost and Luna/Moon had walked off.

Fork came out with the room keys and Jag and I helped transfer Jas's things over to their truck. The Ops were heading home in the morning and so were we after one other stop.

Chapter Fourteen

Devil

"Did you check on Ghost? Is he ready to roll?" Jag asked while we put our things in the saddlebags.

"Yeah, I knocked. He said he'd be out in a couple minutes."

The Ops walked out of their rooms with stuff in hand and went to their truck and threw the bags in the back. As they were making their way over to us, Ghost's door opened and he and Moon walked out. I noticed the difference in the big man immediately. He looked more relaxed than he had been since we met him. I could understand that feeling. And I wanted to get back to it.

"Ride safe. Jas, we're going to miss you around the club. Especially Shakes and Dare. Take care, okay?" Jag said, and Jas walked over and hugged him, then she turned to me and did the same thing.

"Tell Crusher and Stroker, thanks for watching out for Jas. Her momma's appreciative and so are the Ops," Fork said, and then we all shook hands. No one said anything, but we watched as Ghost and Moon whispered to each other, and then she got in the truck as he headed toward us.

"Our pleasure, Jas was great to have around. Take care. You guys call if you need anything else, and we'll keep in touch if we hear anything."

"That works." Fork saluted as he and Cajun headed to their bikes. The women and Jas were in the truck and pulled out first, with the men behind. We watched until they were out of sight.

"If you guys are ready, let's roll, too. I'd like to get this shit handled and back on the road and headed for home," I said, and Ghost and Jag agreed.

I mounted and punched in the address into my GPS that the dipshit texted me and we pulled out. If I got this shit taken care of and we got back on the road, I would be back with Bailey by Thursday night. I smiled; it sounded like a plan.

<hr />

"This place isn't livable for a dog, Dev. If it is an animal he's keeping for her, we got to take it with us."

"Great, it can be the Black Hawk mascot." Jag and I walked up the overgrown path to the front door of a tiny house that looked like it should have been condemned about thirty years ago. Ghost sat in the truck on the street to watch the bikes. The neighborhood was definitely one of those by the time you came out of a place, your shit was up on cinder blocks and stripped. The TV blared from inside, and the wood door stood open. A screen door was the only thing keeping people out. I pounded on the frame and hoped the last hinge didn't break on the door.

I couldn't see anything from the door. A small wall was there, blocking my view so you couldn't see into the living room. Jag walked over to the window and leaned over the bushes and looked through a crack from where the drapes weren't pulled closed tight.

"There's a kid sitting on the couch watching TV. It looked like a girl, but hard to tell through the dirt on the window and on the kid. Let's walk around back and see if there's another door. I wouldn't be surprised if the strung-out fucker didn't text the wrong address."

We signaled to Ghost, and he nodded, then we headed around the side of the house. When we reached the back, another doorway was there, and the door stood open like it did in the front. The TV could still be heard, just not as loud. The tiny backyard was a mess of weeds and trash. I guess drugs are more important than a decent place to live.

I looked in the back door and saw a man sitting at the table eating out of a bowl with a laptop sitting in front of him that was probably worth more than the house.

I knocked on the door, and the man looked over his shoulder and then pushed back his chair and stood. Jag stood off to the side out of sight.

"How much you looking to buy? I'm low right now, but I've got a drop tonight and will have more if you want to come back."

"Fucker, I'm not here to buy drugs. Is this Desiree's place?" The man looked me up and down, then pushed the screen door open.

"You Des's boy?"

"I wouldn't go that far, but we share blood. I'm not here to talk. What the hell do you have of hers that I would be interested in? And I'm going ahead and putting it out there that I won't be paying any fucking bail for her either." I stepped in, and Jag moved in behind me. The man's eyes went back and forth between us.

"They got her down at county lockup for now. She's got a court-appointed lawyer. Stupid bitch is going to go up for a few years this time. Sold to a fucking undercover in a sting, took him to her car because he asked for more than she was carrying. I've told her a hundred times never to take them to the car. Bitch don't listen."

"I don't give a shit about that. Why did you contact me? Only time Desiree does is when she is strapped and needs money. I've never given her any, so I don't know why you would think I would give you shit." The slimy bastard smirked at me, and I stepped toward him, but Jag put his hand on my arm, and I stopped.

"You'll pay or I'm sure I can find another buyer?" I balled my fist, and Jag spoke for the first time.

"Asshole, quit talking in circles and spit it the fuck out before I let the man beat it out of you. How do little pricks like you even live?"

"Because I sell what people want—pussy and drugs. Whatever their pleasure. Now let's talk money since you want to get right down to business. Desiree has been locked up for a week. She had my product confiscated, and she hasn't brought in her weekly take from working the street. Add to that the fact I've been supplying food, power, and water for three and half years, I'd say thirty thousand would be a nice round number. You'd be getting it at a steal considering I could get double, even triple, that price with the right buyer."

"Let's go, Jag. This was a waste of time. That woman doesn't own anything worth that price." I'd heard enough. I turned toward the door that we came in.

"I hungie," followed by the asshole's, "Get your fucking ass back in the living room, Leech!" was my breaking point. Who the hell talked to their kids like that?

Before Jag could move, I had the asshole up against the wall by his neck with his feet dangling.

"Pieces of shit like you should have plastic bags put over their head in the middle of the street and used as an example."

"Dev?" Jag said my name, but I wasn't quite ready to let the man go. He clawed at my hand around his neck and struggled to breathe. Right before I saw the panic in his eyes from not getting any air, I let loose, and he fell to the floor. I stepped back and turned to Jag.

"I wasn't going to kill him." Jag looked at me, then did a chin lift to the doorway leading into the main part of the house. A little girl stood there with stringy, dirty, light brown hair. She wore a t-shirt a size too small, and her jean shorts were filthy. She had dirt streaks on her face, arms, and legs, and was barefoot. Her eyes were a soft brown, and they were looking right at me. But instead of being scared, she just stared.

The idiot on the ground was coughing and holding his throat. Jag moved over by him while I walked to the little girl and kneeled in front of her.

"Hi, sweetheart. Sorry, I hurt your daddy, but I got mad because he was ugly to you." She blinked at me and smiled.

"Leech isn't my daughter," the asshole said and then went into a coughing fit.

I smiled back at the little girl. "Well, that's one good thing going for you in life."

The man sat up and leaned against the wall. "She can be yours for thirty thousand."

Shit. The little girl was Desiree's, making her my half-sister. I looked over at Jag, and he shrugged.

"How old is she?"

"I knew you would be interested. Leech is three and a half. Des don't know the daddy; it was one of her johns."

"If you call her Leech one more time, I'm going to pull your tongue out and shove it up your ass. Got me?" I spoke to the man but kept smiling at the little girl, my sister. Surreal.

"Dev, we've got your back, brother. What you want to do?"

"She comes with us, then I will go see Desiree and have a little chat."

"I'm going to need my thirty thousand in cash."

I pinched the bridge of my nose and shook my head. And Jag actually chuckled. I dropped my hand from my face when the little girl giggled. There was no way she knew what we were talking about. If I thought how the first three plus years of her life had been, I would lose my shit, so I looked forward instead. For my sanity and her future.

"What's your name, sweetheart?"

"Neely. Her name is Neely."

Not responding to the asshole, I stood, and so did Jag.

"Want to grab some of her stuff from the house to take?" Jag asked.

"No. I don't want her to have anything to remind of here." I looked down at Neely. "Want to come with me, sweetheart? I'm your brother. I promise to take care of you, and no one will ever hurt you." I held my hand out and waited to see if she would take it on her own. I planned to take her with us no matter what, but if I could do it without her screaming and drawing attention to us when we walked out, all the better.

"You're not taking her. I'll call the cops. You tried to kill me. I want my money."

I glanced at the asshole. "I don't know your name, and I don't care. But listen to me, really listen because I'm only going to say this once. Neely is going with me. You aren't getting thirty large for her. And you won't call the cops, but if you decide to—before they close the cell door on me, the cops will find your body skinned, and every stash of whatever drug you peddle will be shoved in every orifice your body has." Jag smiled when we looked down at the man; his pants were wet, and he sat in a puddle of his own making.

"Come on, Neely, let's go." She didn't grab my hand, instead she held her tiny dirty arms up. I bent and picked her up, and I didn't look back. People didn't give little kids enough credit, they picked up on more than most thought.

We reached the truck, and when I opened the back door, Ghost looked at me and his eyebrow cocked.

"Meet my sister, Neely, Ghost, and the newest Black Hawk MC family member."

"Hey, darlin'. Bet you were surprised as your brother."

"You got no idea, Ghost." I chuckled.

"We are going to have to just strap her in until we go to a store and pick some things up for her. Starting with one of those seat things," Jag said.

"Yeah, and a lot of other things." I looked at Ghost. "Going to need your help, Ghost. You're the only one out of us to have knowledge about a kid. Jag and I have been around Ally, that's it."

"Sure, I'll help." Ghost forced a smile, and I knew I'd made him think of his son he'd lost in an accident along with his wife.

"Thanks, brother." Ghost nodded in reply.

"Can I suggest a motel closer to the courthouse? You are taking paperwork with you when you see your mom, right?"

"Yeah. Let's get Neely settled. She said inside she was hungry. We can pick up food, then go to the store and get stuff for her. She's going to need to be cleaned up, and that is going to be interesting." Ghost laughed as I fastened the seatbelt around Neely. "Hit GPS and find us a place to stay, Ghost. Jag and I will be behind you."

After he agreed, I smiled at Neely, and she smiled back, then I closed the door and got on my bike and Jag got on his. When Ghost pulled out, we were right behind him.

How the plan for the day had changed?

Chapter Fifteen

Devil

Neely sat in a chair at the table in our motel room and ate her chicken nugget McDonald's Happy Meal. The way she was putting the food away, I wondered when she ate last.

With a washcloth and soap from the bathroom, I'd washed her face and hands so she could eat, but I waited for Jag and Ghost to come back from the store with some clothes and bath items for her. At least Ghost knew what to buy because Jag had no clue, like me.

I'd called my dad and talked to him and then called Crusher. As our Prez, he needed to know because we'd be staying in San Jose until everything was settled. I called Coast and asked for a favor. Being a friend and my brother, he jumped right in. He'd set it up and wait for my text for when we were headed home.

Fucker wanted to sell my sister. See how he liked it when the Feds came calling and his laptop held child pornography and even a few posts where he tried to hook up with a few underage girls. All not traceable back to Black Hawk. Everything originating from him. The inmates were going to love him when he got there.

Jag had been on the phone calling in favors until he left with Ghost. Everyone was pitching in to help me bring my sister home.

"Done, Dev." I looked away from my phone and smiled at Neely. She hadn't said much since we'd been in the room. We'd told her our names, and she could say Dev, but we chuckled when she said Jags and Goss.

"Sweetheart, you are wearing more of that milk than you drank." She looked down at her shirt and swiped her hand over it as if she could wipe it all away. It didn't matter, anyway. Once the guys came back with new clothes, what she was wearing was going into the trash. Nothing from her time in San Jose would be brought to Black Hawk.

"TV?" Neely asked, and I grabbed the remote and turned it on. Found the cartoon channel, and she crawled up on the bed and sat. I got up and walked over to stretch out on the other bed in the room. I closed my eyes and thought of Bailey. I texted her but didn't tell her about Neely. I only told her I would be in San Jose for a few more days, maybe a week.

Neely needed my focus now, and I wanted to tell Bailey in person. My life changed with one stop I hadn't wanted to make in the first place. I had no regrets about that, but Bailey hadn't signed up for it. It had to be her choice. I'd give it to her, but face to face.

The knocking on the door woke me, and when I tried to move to sit up, my arm didn't move. I looked over, and Neely laid across my arm, her head on the pillow, and her body up against mine.

I eased my arm from under her and got out of bed and went to the door. When I opened it, Jag and Ghost came in, each with bags in both hands. They looked over at the bed and saw Neely was asleep, so they set the bags on the other bed.

"I already put the car seat in the truck and got rid of the box. We grabbed kids' shampoo, soap, brush, toothbrush. And every bathroom related item they had. Then we bought tennis shoes, underwear, sock, pants, and shirts." Ghost pointed to Jag. "The VP is responsible for the other charge on your credit card." I looked at Jag and lifted a Harley bag.

"Seriously, you went to a Harley store and bought her clothes?" I shook my head. He opened the bag and pulled out items.

"Hey, she needed a Harley outfit. All biker chicks do."

"Brother, she is three and a half." Ghost and I laughed when Jag sneered.

"Pretty."

The three of us looked over at the bed, and Neely was sitting up looking at the pink t-shirt Jag held in his hands.

"See, age don't matter when it comes to biker babes." We laughed, and Neely joined in.

"Potty, Dev." Neely got down from the bed and walked into the bathroom. Ghost, Jag, nor I moved.

"Does she need help?" Jag asked, and I shrugged, silently praying that she didn't. Ghost shook his head.

"She should, though. She might need help from time to time with buttons or snaps on her pants. Oh, and when she poops, she still might need help with cleaning her butt."

"Oh, hell no. I'm not touching my little sister's bootie or anything else in that area." Jag and Ghost burst out laughing.

"How the hell do you expect her to take a bath? It's no different than anyone else. Dev, you are going to have to wash your sister, or at least help her until she can do it herself."

"This has to be wrong."

"You've washed women before. Think of her as a tiny woman." Ghost and I both jerked our heads toward Jag. "What?"

"VP, that was a poor comparison," Ghost commented.

Jag's eyes got big when he realized what he'd said. "Fucking, pervs. Just the washing part of a woman—not the reason you wash a grown woman. Ew, sick bastards."

"Dev! I pooped!" I froze, and Jag and Ghost bent over laughing. "Come on, I'll pay one of you?" Both their heads shook. "Fine, but I don't know who is going to be traumatized more in the future when she is a teenager and remembers her brother wiped and washed he..." I couldn't bring myself to finish the sentence. Ghost and Jag laughed harder, and I glared.

"Dev! I pooped!"

"Coming, Neely!" I yelled, then to Jag and Ghost I said, "Dickheads." I headed toward the bathroom. We were going to learn together. The Good, the Bad, and the Ugly. I hoped Neely's and my future didn't play out like the movie.

A few days turned into five, and I found out that living in a motel room with a little girl was worse than a thirteen-mile hike in full battle gear. I also learned along with Jag, which had been funny at the time, not so much when it was me, that with short humans your jewels needed to be protected. That only took one time to learn.

The line moved and brought me out of my thoughts and back to where I stood to wait my turn to be frisked. County lockup, fucking fantastic. They moved us through pretty quickly, and then I was put in a room to wait for them to bring Desiree in. One of the favors asked for.

When the door opened and Desiree walked in with her guard, she smiled and then moved to the seat across the table from me.

"I'll be outside the door if you need me," the guard said.

"Good, we won't be long." The guard nodded and walked out.

"You've grown into a handsome man, Lance," Desiree said, and looked me over. Her hair was dull brown, and her green eyes sunken. She had dark circles under her eyes, and her face was pocked and broke out from all the drugs. When she smiled earlier, her teeth showed the signs of meth use.

"This isn't a reunion, Desiree. I've brought paperwork for you to sign relinquishing your parental rights over Neely."

"What happens if I don't want to?"

"I will fight you in court for her. It will take a little longer, but I will win. You're going to serve time and not just a few months, so I will win easy enough. Don't be selfish, Desiree. You had two chances to be a mother. Some women don't even get one. And you failed both times." I pushed the papers across the table. "Look them over, but sign when you're done. When you are ready to sign, the guard can witness it. Already cleared that with the courts here."

She picked up the papers and looked over them and asked a question that had been bugging me about Neely.

"How did she not get taken away from you when she was born? No way would they have let you out of a hospital with a baby addicted to drugs." She sat the papers down and sat her hands down on top of them.

"I was clean and only hooking when I got pregnant with her. I was shocked when I went to the clinic, and they told me I was pregnant. I was forty-five. After she was born, I met Ernie, and he was easy to work with. Didn't take as big of a cut as some of the other pimps, plus I could make extra cash selling product. So, Neely wasn't born addicted to answer your question. I didn't start using again until she was like three months."

"Well, that is something you gave her. Are you ready to sign? I need to get the guard in here."

"Preacher—" I stuck my hand up and cut her off.

"I will not listen to you talk about my dad. You could tell me he slapped you around, killed in cold blood, and I wouldn't give two shits. He is the one who sat with me while the drugs worked out of my system. He is the one who raised me. My mother couldn't stay clean long enough to give birth. You don't get to say his name. You are proof that not all women are born with mothering instincts. Once those papers are signed, you are not to contact us. You will never see Neely grow up, nothing. Preacher was there for me, and I will be there for her. Your job as a mother is over for both Neely and I as soon as you sign on the dotted line."

I got up and knocked on the door, and the guard came in.

"She's ready for you to witness her signature."

The guard handed her a pen and stood beside her as she flipped the pages to get to the last one where she needed to sign. She paused with the pen over the paper.

"Sign it, Desiree. Give Neely one thing while you are still her mother—a better life."

Desiree Locke signed the paperwork, stood, and walked out with the guard. I leaned back in the chair and took a deep breath. One more thing completed to get my life on track.

Jag needed to file the paperwork and get whatever else done to go along with it. I was just relieved that when all was said and done, and we rode home to Black Hawk, where the one thing to complete my life was.

Chapter Sixteen

Bailey

"Almost two weeks and all I get are texts at night telling me he loves me and hopes I will understand. Who says shit like that in a text?" I pulled the clean paper down on the exam table and set out a new tray.

"Are you going to tell me what is going on with you? You've mumbled to yourself all week. Are you not happy working here?" Mac asked. I hadn't told her about anything because how could I when I didn't know myself what the fuck was going on.

"Sorry. Lance has been gone for almost two weeks. He is supposed to be back sometime today, and he said he would let me know because we needed to talk, and he hopes I will understand."

"Understand what?" Mac asked.

"Exactly! He wouldn't say. Said it had to be in person."

"Okay. Have you asked Sami and Carly if they know what is going on?"

"Yes, and they don't know, or they can't say. They said Lance wanted to talk to me and that Crusher and Speed told them to butt out. I didn't want to put them in the middle, so I didn't push."

"Are you going to Black Hawk and wait for him?"

"He said he would call me if he weren't going to be too late getting in. If not, he would call me in the morning."

"And you are going to listen, why?"

"I don't know. What if he found another woman? What if he changed his mind? What if he doesn't want to be with me? I don't think I can handle it." Mac burst out laughing, and I frowned at her.

"Girlfriend, you sound like a crazy person. That man loves you. It shows in his eyes, Bailey."

"What if he doesn't love me enough?"

"What is enough?" Mac smiled at me.

"See? He makes me crazy and mad. He makes me happy and then does something I would like to kill him for."

"That, Bailey, sounds like *enough* love."

Mac and I finished the day, and I had officially worked as an RN for one week. I went home, showered, and shoved a few things into a bag. I was going to Black Hawk and sit on Lance's porch until he came home.

I had discussed everything with my mom and got almost the same responses as I'd gotten from Mac.

The road to turn into Black Hawk came into view, and when I pulled up to the gate, a younger man stood there. One I had never met.

"What can I do for you, ma'am?"

"I'm here to see Lance. I mean Devil. I'm his umm... girlfriend."

"What's your name?"

"Bailey Tolson." The man looked down at the clipboard in his hand, then looked at me.

"Sorry, can't let you in. You aren't listed as an automatic entry, Ms. Tolson."

I felt my temper rise as the man walked off.

"Can you call someone? Sami, Carly, one of the other members?"

"I'll call Devil if you can wait?"

"He is back?"

The man pulled out his cell and started scrolling.

"Yes, Devil, the girl, Jag, and Ghost pulled in about thirty minutes ago." When the man didn't look up, I threw the car in drive and went right through the opened gate. I figured they could haul my ass off later.

The prospect at the gate had his phone at his ear, so I was sure someone would know I was coming.

When I reached Lance's house, his dad stepped out onto the porch. By the time the man stepped down to open my door, I was out of the car and moving toward him.

"Hey, Bailey. Good to see you. Lance hadn't gotten a chance to text you—"

"I just bet he hasn't." I interrupted Preacher and moved around him, stomped up the few steps, and entered Lance's house. I slammed the door shut on Preacher's "Wait."

"Devil and the girl. Yeah, he wanted to talk in person. What a big old crock of shit. Lance!" I mumbled the beginning, then yelled out his name. I heard footsteps upstairs, then saw him as he started down. He smiled at me, and I wanted to rip his lips right off his face.

"Can you keep it down? Neely was exhausted from the trip, and she's asleep."

"Oh, let's not wake a tired Neely. She needs her sleep. I suppose you were laying down with Neely?"

"Yeah. What is your problem, Bay? Sorry, I didn't text or call right when I pulled in, but I had to get Neely settled. I was going to text after she fell asleep, but Vic called from the gate and said you were on your way."

"Well, of course, Vic did. I wasn't on the entry list!"

"I told you to lower your voice. You are acting crazy."

"Oh, wouldn't want you to have to deal with a little crazy." I turned to leave.

"Dev?" I swung back around at the child's voice.

"Hold on, sweetheart." I stood and watched as Lance trotted up the stairs and grabbed the little girl up and started back down.

"So Neely has a little girl?" I asked, and Lance frown at me, and the little girl stared.

"No, *this* is Neely. What are you talking about, Bailey? My dad went outside to tell you. Did you not see him?"

"Uh... I sort of blew him off and stormed in because I thought you had a woman in here." Lance chuckled and looked at the little girl.

"Neely, I think Bay was jealous."

The little girl laid her head on Lance's shoulder, and I melted. She was the cutest thing I'd ever seen.

"Bay, I'd like you to meet my sister, Neely. She's what I wanted to talk about. She's also why I stayed gone for almost two weeks. You know my story with my mom. I had to take her, Bailey. So, I wanted to see you face to face to tell you everything. It's not just me anymore, Bay. Neely comes as part of the package too. You started a new job, and so many things have happened—"

"Shut up, Lance. That angel needs to go back to bed. She looks exhausted." I moved closer to Neely, and her eyes followed me. When I stood in front of her and Lance, I held my arms out. "Let's go lay down, sweetie." Neely let go of Lance and came to me. When I put her on my hip, she laid her head down on my shoulder like she had done with Lance.

I started up the stairs, and Lance followed. When we reached the guest bedroom, I was shocked. The room was done in pink and accented with Harley items. Even the blanket on the bed was done in Harley pink.

"The women of the club. My dad and the others. They wanted her to have her own stuff when she got here." Lance's phone chimed, and he pulled it out of his pocket while I went to the bed and laid Neely down. She was out. I turned back and pushed on Lance to shove him out the door because he was chuckling.

"What's so funny?" I asked him as we stepped into the hall.

"Dad texted and said he didn't come back in because he wanted us to have time alone.

"Aww, that is sweet."

"You wouldn't say that if you read the sentence after. It said because you are crazy." Lance laughed and shoved the phone back in his pocket and reached down and grabbed my hand and started leading me to his bedroom.

"Really? Do you think you can solve everything with sex?"

"Well, I was just going to ask you to lie down with me because I'm exhausted, but since you brought it up."

Lance walked me into his room and closed the door.

"I brought a bag with me. It's in the car. Let me go get it." I turned toward the door, and he grabbed me around my waist, and before I knew what was going on, I hit the bed with a bounce.

"You don't need the bag right now. Strip."

"Now who is crazy?" I chuckled but stopped when Lance started taking off his clothes.

"I'm ripping anything left on your body when I'm finished."

I kneeled on the bed and rushed to get my clothes off before he was done. My panties were the only thing left when he stood before me naked.

"Missed you, Bay," Lance said and lunged. Before I could react, I heard the rip of material, and my panties were thrown over his shoulder.

Chapter Seventeen

Devil

"So sweet," I whispered, and kissed her inner thigh. Bailey squirmed a little and then settled down while I spread her legs enough to lie between them. Shit, I couldn't believe I was going to have a lifetime of this with her. She moaned with the first swipe of my tongue, and I worked her pussy until she bucked, wanting more. Begging for more with words barely recognizable.

Using my hands, I parted the soft skin and focused on her clit. I sucked it into my mouth and flicked it with my tongue. When I bit down gently on the nub, Bailey's hand went to her mouth. She was trying to be quiet, which she seemed to be having difficulty doing.

My cock pulsed, but it was going to have to wait its turn. I wanted Bailey's first orgasm with my mouth. After close to two weeks away, I wanted to coat my tongue with the taste of her.

How had I stayed away from Bailey? I would always regret the time lost with her.

I pumped a finger in and out of her while I continued to flick her clit with my tongue, and when I felt her body tremble and she started to tighten around my finger, I pulled my fingers out and used my tongue to finish her off. She came hard, fast, and I lapped, catching everything she gave me on my tongue.

"Lance," Bailey said after she removed the hand from her mouth and then wiggled her hips a little.

"You need some more, baby? Need my cock? While I was gone, did your pussy miss being filled?" I moved up her body, then leaned down and kissed her, letting her taste herself on my tongue.

I held Bailey's hips and slowly entered her as I kissed her deeply. She groaned when I was fully seated. I pulled back and smiled against her mouth as I grounded my hips against hers.

I moved slowly at first, then picked up speed. I moved faster, and Bailey worked her hips, keeping pace with me. I braced my hands on the bed, pushed myself up a little. The move brought my hips down, so with each pass, my cock brushed against her engorged clit. Bailey panted and bit her lip, doing everything to keep from screaming.

Though I moved faster and faster, she stayed with me stroke for stroke, and I groaned when I felt my orgasm building. My balls were drawing up as I felt her slick walls clamp down, locking me in their confines. I knew it was the end. I gritted my teeth and buried my face into Bailey's neck as she pulled us both over the edge.

I lifted my head and looked at Bailey's face. She was beautiful, and I would be grateful every day for the second chance I'd been given.

I collapsed against her and again buried my head in her neck. Bailey wrapped her arms around me and stroked her fingers down my back.

We were both slick with sweat, and I felt her shiver from the cool air. I pulled out from her body and shifted to lie down beside her.

As she laid on the bed in a sexual daze and breathing hard, I took advantage.

"Marry me, Bailey?" I asked and waited while she tried to get her breathing under control.

"Lance, it's all so fast."

"Jump with me, Bay. Take a chance. Let me love you for the next fifty-plus years. Help me raise Neely."

The room fell into silence and when I almost had gave up hope, the whispered, "Yes," reached my ears.

I faced her not only so I could see her face, but she could see mine. "I love you, Bay."

"I love you, too, Lance."

We laid there, closing our eyes, and enjoying the quietness. As sleep started pulling at me, I had one more thing to let her know.

"See, I can get what I want with sex." The pop to the chest made me laugh.

"You're such an asshole." I pulled her tight and rested my cheek against the top of her head.

Once again, I wondered how the fuck I ever thought I could live without her.

Epilogue

Jag

"Yo, Jag!" I heard Speed yell from outside the garage.

"What's up?" I yelled back as I wiped the oil that covered my hands on a rag and stepped out of the garage.

"Sami was supposed to go to the courthouse and file the final papers on the sale of her house in town, then she was going to drop by there to meet the woman who bought it, but she's not feeling well. Think you could do it and then meet the woman at the house to give her the keys and her copy of the documents?"

"Sure. Let me run by my house and change into some clean clothes, then I'll stop by and grab the paperwork from you."

"Uh... morning sickness is kicking Sami's ass. She was supposed to be meeting the woman in twenty."

"Shit, okay." I looked down at the worn jeans streaked with grease and at the black t-shirt that was in no better shape. No way would I be able to get changed, drive to the courthouse, and be at the house in twenty minutes. Well, nothing I could do about it. "Grab the paperwork while I at least finish washing my hands, and I'll meet you by my bike." I turned back into the garage as Speed went in the door to his house.

In less than five minutes, I was on my bike, pulling out on the main road toward town. The ride was enjoyed as always, but I was definitely going to be late. Hopefully, the woman would understand that shit happens. When I reached the courthouse parking lot, it was full. I circled and was on my second trip around the lot when I noticed a car backing out of a spot one row over. As I reached the spot, a Mercedes Benz Cabriolet whipped in, barely missing my front tire. Fuck, if I hadn't been paying attention and hit my brakes, the damn asshole driving would have mowed me down.

I pulled up behind the car, killed the engine, and shoved the kickstand down. When I dismounted and skirted the rear, a woman had already gotten out and was walking toward the courthouse.

"Where the hell did you learn to drive?" I yelled, and she stopped and turned.

"Excuse me?"

"Excuse you? You act as if you didn't just cut me off to take the parking spot. Lady, if I hadn't been paying attention, you would have hit me. No way in hell you didn't see me."

"Oh please, I saw the spot first." She eyed me up and down, curled her lip as though she didn't like what she saw, then threw her chin out and continued. "I'm running late and don't have time to argue with you. You have a motorcycle, it will fit anywhere," she said and waved her hand toward my bike and then turned and started walking again.

"Hey, don't walk away when I'm talking to you!"

"Your parole officer and/or public defender are probably waiting for you. Good luck in court!" she yelled over her shoulder.

"What a bitch," I muttered as I watched her move across the lot, pull the door open, and walk into the building.

Well, she was right about one thing: my bike would fit almost anywhere, especially since her little car was pulled all the way up into the spot. I walked back to my bike and proceeded to position it as close to the tail end of her car as I could get. She was going to talk to me one way or another.

I grabbed the paperwork out of my saddlebag and headed to the courthouse. As I walked, I rechecked the documents to make sure everything was there. They were in order and the only thing left was to get them date stamped, and the deed filed with the clerk.

Fifteen minutes later, I was in the parking lot and relaxed against the hood of the woman's car. The wait for her wasn't long, and since I had cooled off a little, I got to appreciate the look of her when she pushed the door to the courthouse open and stepped out onto the sidewalk. She had a mess of red hair that was piled on top of her head and held in place with something I couldn't see. Plus, at the distance where I sat, I couldn't make out her eye color either, but her body—now that was a different story.

The black pants looked tailor-fitted and matched the jacket and white blouse she wore underneath. The woman had an air about her. She stopped and pulled a cell phone out of her bag and after punching a few keys; she placed it up to her ear, that's when she looked up and noticed me. She squinted her eyes and started walking toward me as she talked to whoever was on the other end of her call. When she reached me, she mumbled into the phone, then hung up. The eyes that flashed anger toward me were a dark shade of green and set in a classically beautiful face.

Damn, since I hadn't noticed how gorgeous she was the first time, only showed the degree of mad I had been in. No way I would have missed this woman the first go around.

"What? Did they not have enough evidence to keep you? And why is your butt on the hood of my car?" With that haughty voice, I didn't know if I wanted to turn her over my knee and spank her ass or grab her by the shoulders and pull her into my body and kiss her. I stood from the relaxed position, which brought my body closer to her, and I'd give her credit, she didn't step back like most would have. Instead, she tilted her head back and looked up at me.

"Drivers like you are the reason we end up eating the pavement. Ya think you own the f'n road." This had to be the most absurd encounter. The woman had pissed me off before. Now, I wanted to get under her skin.

"Seriously? You," she looked me over again, then continued, "are going to give me lessons on driving because I reached a parking space first?"

"First? Hell, I was at the spot when you whipped in front of me to take it."

"Oh, for Pete's sakes, I do not have time to stand here and debate with you. I have another appointment. Why don't you get your death machine out of my way?" She moved to go around me, and I shifted, blocking her.

"Never been on a bike before, darlin'? You don't know what you're missing pressed against your man's back, the vibration of the bike between your thighs. Maybe I should take you for a ride. It might loosen you up and thaw you out."

"You are all the same. Everything revolves around your penis. I'm not frozen. I just have taste and respect for myself." This time when she went to go around me, I allowed it. I turned as she used her remote to shut the alarm off and unlock the door before she reached for the handle.

"Goddamn, is it me or all men? Women like you are the reason men swear to never marry or end up filing for divorce," I said as I walked past her and got on my bike, starting it up. My words stopped her just as she was getting in the car.

She yelled over the sound of my bike, "Can't argue with you on that—I just picked up my final decree!" Then she slid the rest of the way into her car and started it.

Well... shit.

Acknowledgements

Thank you to all the readers who waited patiently for Devil's book. If anything; he was true to his name as he teased, then would change how he wanted his story told.

I hope you enjoy it half as much as I wanted to kill him for being a pain in the butt. Which was a lot!

Carson

About the Author

Carson Mackenzie enjoys writing romance with a real feel inside the stories. She writes with the belief not every man is a jerk and not every woman needs saving.

Carson lives in the South with one of her sons, a Great Dane and two adopted shelter dogs that keep the household in line. Books have always been a part of her life. There is nothing better to her than curling up and relaxing with a good story and losing herself in someone else's world for a few hours.

Writing stories and growing as an author with each book is her goal. She wants to reach the level where a reader knows when they see her name, they can trust in the fact there will be a good story as they flip through the pages.

Carson's been her writing journey for a few years. As she's finally starting to settle in, her only regret is she hadn't started sooner.

To stay up to date with Carson – visit her website- https://carsonmackenzieauthor.com/ or sign up for her newsletter- https://landing.mailerlite.com/webforms/landing/l2k1l8.

Books by Carson Mackenzie

Black Hawk MC

Speed
Crusher
Devil
Ghost
Jag
Coast
Flirt

Haven MC

Moose's Regret
Hawk's Bounty
Keg's Revelation

Desert Phoenix MC

Desert Phoenix Rising

Standalones

Her Way or No Way
two paths One destiny

Boxed Sets

Black Hawk MC Books 1-3
Black Hawk MC Books 4-7
Haven MC Books 1-3